Pulse of Life

A Collection of Short Stories and Poetry

Laois Writers Group

Published in 2011 by

Laoise Writers Group

Ballylehaun House

Gathabawn

County Kilkenny

ISBN No: 978-0-9570899-0-7

A CIP catalogue for this book is available from

The British Library

Cover design by Graciela Ryan

Printed by Donovan Printing Ltd

Newbridge, Co. Kildare

Tel: 045 433874/435288

All proceeds of the sales of this book to the

Cuisle Centre, Block Road, Portlaoise.

Acknowledgements

I would like to thank the members of the Laois Writers Group, for their creative efforts captured in the pages of this anthology.

To Dan and Mary Carmody of the Mile Bush, Portlaoise, who hosted our Table Quiz and continue to host our meetings every Thursday night, many thanks.

A special thank you to Jack and Ciara Nolan, without whom our table quiz night, would ever have happened.

To our sponsors who are listed on the back page of this anthology, especially Laois County Council, Dept. of the Environment, VHI Staff Charities Committee, the siblings of Anthony O'Sullivan, and the fundraising efforts of Tom Moore and Mary Conway, many thanks to all, in appreciation of their generosity.

I would like to thank Graciela Ryan for her expertise in the layout, formatting and cover design of this anthology, for her design of our Book Publication and Pub Quiz posters, and for her patience in the face of my ignorance.

Last but not least, a very special thanks to Dan Carmody for his editing skills, printing and media know how.

Margaret Cotter

Chairperson Laois Writers Group

Foreword

It gives me great pleasure to invite you to read the first anthology from the Laois Writers Group.

Words are the way we communicate with one another. Through them we give voice to our thoughts and emotions. They come in many different languages and they can be as elaborate and colourful, or plain and simple as we desire.

The voices in this book are rich and varied, coming not only from Kerry, Dublin, and the midlands, but also from Mexico and Great Britain. They draw deep from the well of life, sharing childhood reminiscences, and stories handed down through family history. They speak of birth, death, of love shared and lost, of famine, war, and the beauty of nature in all its forms and seasons.

Sometimes sad, sometimes funny, these authors combine their own experiences and their fertile imaginations, to weave a rich tapestry stitch by stitch, as they take us through the pages of this book.

Margaret Cotter

Contents

A DRAMATIC AFFAIR

I was sorry I hadn't phoned Mary to see if she would be at home before I started the long walk up her driveway. It was a pitch dark night and I felt very uneasy. The branches of the overhanging trees were like spectral fingers reaching down to grab me. There were strange scurrying and rustlings in the undergrowth, which set my heart racing. I quickened my step anxious to get indoors. Finally I rounded the corner of the drive and found the house ablaze with light. Gasping with relief I ran towards the front door.

The sitting room curtains were parted and I had a clear view of the room. I reeled in shock.

Mary lay the full length of the couch, and draped across her was the local Garda Sergeant. He still sported his cap so he must have been in a hurry! Mary wasn't making any attempt to dislodge him so I presumed she was enjoying herself.

Disappointed and not a little shocked I turned away, dreading the walk back down the dark drive and another lonely night of just my own company. As I hurried back along the drive, I heard the crunch of feet on the gravel. I peered into the darkness shaking with fear as a tall shadowy figure materialised before me.

"Goodnight Chris, this is a surprise," the figure said in the unmistakable voice of Mary's husband.

For a minute I was stunned, and then my brain went into top gear. I couldn't let him find Mary. I pretended to be scared. "Oh John, I'm so glad to see you," I allowed my voice to wobble. "I'm so scared, I've been up to the house to ask Mary's help but she's not in. You see," I explained, "when I got home from work I saw that the light was on in my bedroom. I know I didn't leave it on myself and I'm frightened of going into the house on my own."

John couldn't know that I left on the light every morning as a deterrent for any would-be thieves. He put a comradely arm around my shoulders and agreed to accompany me home. "Despite what you say, Chris, I bet you left the light on yourself," he said as I turned the key in the lock.

We had a look around the kitchen, "nothing seems to be disturbed here anyway," he commented, "everything looks ship-shape to me." Nevertheless he took the poker from the fireplace and tested its weight as he turned to me. "I'm going to look upstairs Chris, why don't you make a nice cup of tea for the both of us, you look as if you're suffering from shock and could certainly use one. I'll be back shortly." John searched the three bedrooms upstairs, and of course found nothing amiss.

Later as he sat facing me across the kitchen table he laughed and said. "The old memory is going dear; you must need to relax more often." He finished the tea and made to leave.

I begged him to stay a little longer. "Just until I settle, John, you just don't know how scared I've been."

He looked at his watch. "Right, I'll stay another twenty minutes then I must go. The drama society is rehearsing in our house tonight. Mary is the leading lady and Sergeant Troy is the leading man. I wrote the play myself, it's my first attempt at a play with torrid love scenes, and you can imagine how anxious I am to see them acted out!"

BAD BOY

Early morning, dew still on the grass, as the man approaches, a skylark rises from the meadow, trilling upwards into a clear sky. The sward is looking thick this year, he thinks. It will need to be if next winter is anything like the last. He marvels at the fact that the grass and herbs have grown so well. After all, they were buried in snow from Christmas to Easter. But the summer is proving to be as hot as the winter was cold.

Later, he would hitch his favourite mare to the mowing machine and start cutting. He spent long hours yesterday preparing the machine, sharpening the blades, cleaning and oiling the mechanism.

He remembers how his father taught him to use a scythe. It's different now. Machinery can make so many traditional tasks easier for his generation than for his father's. And it will be easier still, he supposes, for his sons. But he's not ready, yet, to give up using a horse for some tasks. Especially as Dora, the mare has helped him win so many awards for ploughing.

The two rabbits he has killed on his morning walk around the farm hang from his shoulders. Eva will make a nice stew with those.

There's something else he needs the gun for. Not a pleasant task. Bess has been a faithful servant for more years than he cares to remember. She was retired years ago but now it is time for her to be put down before sickness and old age make her life intolerable.

He strides across the farmyard and into the long barn. Empty now, after the long winter, soon it will be filled to the roof with new hay. Just inside the entrance a length of rope dangles from a hook embedded in a timber roof support.

"Darn! Where be the bitch?" He raises his voice to a shout: "Henry! Henry, boy, where are you? What have you done with Bess?"

It does not occur to him that anyone but his youngest son, Henry, could be responsible for the disappearance. Arriving unexpectedly when he and Eva were already middle-aged, doted on by his mother and spoiled by his older siblings, Henry is a constant source of worry for his father. Henry's failure to distinguish himself at the village school was of no great concern. The older man believed that knowledge of "the three Rs" was of limited value to a farmer. He had barely mastered them himself. But he knows a farmer needs other attributes many of which his son seems to lack.

Henry reminds him more than a little of his nephew, Geoffrey. What might have become of Geoffrey if his uncle had not allowed him to graze a few cows on his land was anyone's guess.

And then there was his sister, Anne, a lonely spinster living in a cottage belonging to her brother. Anne spent her days pouring over a bible. Last summer she had been arrested after accosting people in the centre of the town, telling them she was pregnant with the new messiah. The upshot had been a long period under the care of the local mental hospital, from where she had only recently been released. And there had been intimations that Henry may be destined to follow suit.

He hoped it wouldn't come to that but the boy's behaviour of late had become increasingly worrisome. Only yesterday he'd caught him sitting in the dirt between two rows of peas in the vegetable garden. He was supposed to be weeding but had gone into one of those strange reveries to which he was increasingly prone.

On the lane coming back from the common Henry heard his father's shout. He would have been back before now if only Bess would move faster. He'd found her tied up in the long barn and decided to take her with him on his morning walk up the hill behind the farmhouse. He had watched, engrossed, as bees and butterflies buzzed and flitted in the gorse and broom flowers. A family of rabbits skittered out of a burrow and a peewit climbed skywards. Now he was heading back towards home. "I wonder what Dada wants?" He asked himself. Why did his father sound so angry about him having taken Bess on his morning walk? He remembered mornings when his father had taken Bess with him on his own walks. But that had not happened for a while now.

"There you are, boy, and Bess. Give her to me. Now you go on inside. I'm sure there are things you could be doing for Mother."

Something made Henry hesitate before giving his father the free end of the length of binder twine he'd used to lead Bess.

"Here, take these rabbits to your mother. We'll have a tasty stew tonight."

Crossing the farmyard from the long barn towards the house Henry turned to look back at his father.

"Noooo!" Breaking into a run he dropped the rabbits and raced back to the long barn. His father was cocking the gun. Something his father had said yesterday suddenly flamed in his memory.

"No, Dada, no!" He cried as he ran towards his father. His father turned, holding the gun, as Henry ran up to him. Raw emotion lending him surprising strength, Henry tried to wrestle the gun from his father. "No, you can't. You can't."

The explosion was loud. So loud and so close to Henry's right ear that for long seconds all he could hear was a buzzing. His father was on his knees, his hands to his face. Blood oozed between his fingers and he sagged further, collapsing as an awful noise was torn from him.

Henry ran, ignoring the moist warmth that was spreading across the front of his cord trousers. Henry ran.

The noise of the explosion still rang in his ears, but not loudly enough to drown out the dreadful sound of his father's agony.

Henry ran.

His breath came in great sobbing gasps. Through the gate and across the hay meadow he ran, then stopped, "Bess!" Where was his friend?

With relief he saw Bess hobbling after him. "Come on, girl," he said, kneeling and burying his head in the animal's fur.

The women were in the dairy, churning milk. Eva had heard her husband's shout which she ignored. The shot also came as no surprise. She knew of her husband's plans.

"I'd better put the kettle on," she said. "Dada will be in for his morning break directly." Soon the kettle was singing merrily and she poured a measure into the big brown teapot to warm it, swirling the hot liquid around and throwing it into the stone sink. She placed four heaped teaspoons of Ty-Phoo in the pot and added the boiling water. The full pot was placed in the centre of the table that dominated the farmhouse kitchen and covered with a knitted tea cosy.

"Not here yet?" Margery's query was superfluous for it was clear that her father was not present. Stepping towards the kitchen door, the top half of which was opened she called out "Dada!"

No response.

"I'll just go and see where he is," spoken over her shoulder as she descended the three stone steps into the yard. Crossing the farmyard towards the long barn she stopped, transfixed by the scene that greeted her. Then she screamed.

Henry had stopped running. He hadn't stopped shaking. The sobs had subsided, though not completely. He'd stopped running for two reasons. Firstly he didn't know where to go. Finding somewhere to hide would not be difficult. But how would he survive?

He could kill a rabbit. He'd seen it done many times. At harvest time children of all ages would be recruited to help. The main task would be collecting the sheaves, shed by the binder, and arranging them in stocks. But as the binder travelled round the field in laps of decreasing size, as the rectangle of unharvested corn became smaller, the rabbits trapped within it would start to make a desperate bid for freedom.

Then the children, like fieldsmen in some macabre cricket match, would run and pounce upon the escapees. A quick sharp blow, to the back of the head, would break the animal's neck. There'd be plenty of rabbit pies and stews over the next few days.

Henry hated that bit and always gave any rabbit he caught to someone else to kill. But, yes, he knew how to kill a rabbit and, he supposed, if his life depended on it, he could do it. And he could skin it, using the knife his uncle Ivor had given him for his twelfth birthday. It had a beautifully carved ivory handle, two blades and a spike for cleaning horses' hooves. And, like most country boys of his age, he had learned how to tickle a trout – and there would be trout in each of the streams that flowed eastwards from the nearby mountains. But how would he cook either? He had no matches.

The second reason he had stopped running was that he knew there would be plenty of time. There was no phone at the farmhouse so his older brother Cecil would have to drive Dada's car the three miles to the village to get PC Jones and Dr. Mac. He doubted that anyone would think of looking for him until they'd confirmed what he believed to be true. And as the enormity of that truth sank in he began to shake uncontrollably. His mind was flooded with the image of his father's blood oozing from between his fingers. And his ears still rang, not with the sound of the shot, but with the dreadful noise his father had uttered as he sank to the ground.

"I can tell you the damage is mostly superficial," Dr. McCullogh, – affectionately know as "Dr. Mac" by his patients - paused for effect before continuing in his highland brogue. "But you'll almost certainly lose the sight of that eye. I need to get you into the eye hospital. They'll remove the pellets and make a more accurate prognosis than I."

Cecil had not driven to the village. He had gone in the opposite direction, to the doctor's house. He'd followed the doctor back to the farm; the doctor's Rover negotiating the hills and bends at a faster speed than his father's elderly Morris.

By the time the doctor arrived, Margery had helped her father into the kitchen and settled him in his favourite chair, in front of the fire. She'd washed the blood from his face and plied him with cups of her mother's tea to treat the symptoms of shock.

No one had mentioned Henry. And in answer to the doctor's query the old man had said only that he'd tripped and fallen.

"Dangerous things, guns, too easy to become complacent," had been the doctor's response. "You should have that safety catch on all the time."

"I'll go with Dada in the doctor's car," Eva said. "Cecil, you had better follow in the Morris to bring me home in case Dada has to stay in overnight. Margery, you had better stay here to see Henry's ok."

"Where is Henry?" asked Margery, suddenly aware that they had all been too preoccupied with her father's condition to notice that Henry was missing.

Henry was in among the tumbled stone walls that had once been an inn called the King's Arms. Destroyed by fire many years ago the roof timbers and door frames had long since disappeared. Ancient fruit trees sprawled untidily in the small orchard beside it. One, viewed from a certain angle, resembled a gibbet.

Elder bushes had taken root in the walls and these provided some protection from the mid-day sun as he and Bess sat, he with his back to a wall and she with her head in his lap.

Both had slaked their thirst in a nearby stream. Henry was still shaking. Still unable to drive from his memory the terrible image of his father collapsing and the inhuman sound that he had uttered in doing so.

But other memories kept intruding. Like the taunts of fellow pupils when he was at school. "Sissy!" They'd shout, and "you be saft, saft in the ,,ead. That's what you be."

Worst of all was an exchange he'd overheard one day. Unaware that Henry was sitting in a cubicle of the outside toilets two lads were continuing a conversation as they indulged a favourite sport – attempting to piss over the wall into the girl's facility.

"It b'aint right for 'im to be in the same school as us," said one. "That's what my dad do say, any road." There was a pause as the other boy digested this piece of information, then: "Says ,,e ought to be put away. Into one of them special schools, like."

Henry had no idea what being sent away to a special school would entail but he had an instinctive dislike and fear of the idea. His aunt Annie had been sent away last year. People had said she was "saft in the ,,ead". One conversation he'd overheard included the opinion that his aunt "might as well be dead as spend ,,er life in one of them places."

Well, he might as well be dead. He'd killed his father. That was murder, he reasoned. And they hanged murderers didn't they?

They found him at sunset. Margery and Cecil had spent the afternoon and evening searching the land around the farm. As they walked up the lane leading to the King's Arms they saw Bess limping towards them, tongue lolling out and uttering a pitiful whining. Margery squatted to pet the old bitch.

"What's the matter old girl?" She asked. "I'm sure you know where he is. Show us." Then she looked up and uttered the second scream of the day.

MR JINGLES

It was a day in the depths of winter, with temperatures in the minus bracket and all humanity scurrying for shelter and warmth. However weather never deterred my mother of almost ninety, from her afternoon outing. It broke the monotony was her story and my job was what the family described as "Driving Miss Daisy."

With the car heater on max, and mother's knees tucked in a warm rug, we set out, undaunted by the severe weather forecast, for the rest of the day. First stop was the supermarket, where I hastily shopped for mother's essentials. Loading the bags of fresh beef, chicken, milk, cheese, bread and vegetables into the boot, I thought, no fear of it going off in there, giving the freezing temperatures.

Satisfied with our purchases, and in no hurry, we navigated on to the main road where traffic was steady but slow. As we drove along mother related all the latest family news and gossip, culminating in the subject of her health, and how she slept the previous night. When the conversation inevitably brooked on religion and politics, I nodded in agreement, something I had learned from a lifetime's experience of dealing with my mother's strongly held beliefs.

Driving leisurely along, the car warm as toast, and mother's comments down to a minimum, I suddenly saw a movement out of the corner of my eye. I risked another glance and felt my body stiffen and my grip on the steering wheel tighten. "Mam," I said, trying to keep my concentration on the road and the flurries of snow, "look."

Roused from her warm, drowsy state, she glanced quickly around the car. "Look at what?" She replied in an irritated voice, "I don't see anything."

Without turning my head I whispered, "Look straight behind the wheel on the dash board." Sitting there as bold as brass, sat a mouse. Mesmerised, I had a fleeting vision of "Mr. Jingles," the pet mouse in the film "The Green Mile". His two beady eyes looked straight at me and with his ears erect, and his fur blowing gently in the hot air vent, he appeared totally unafraid.

Mother was as ever calm, her only comment being; "well the cheeky little beggar, how did he get in here?"

"Shoo, shoo," I called, banging the side of the door, desperately trying to keep my attention on the poor visibility and slippery roads. Shoo he did but to where? My thoughts turned to the goodies in the boot. The impulse to jam on the brakes and jump out was not an option, given the traffic, and the now heavy fall of snow, only one thing for it, keep going.

The journey home of twenty minutes, took an agonising half an hour, with mother berating me as to my laxity in the general upkeep of my car.

"If you regularly cleaned your car, this would never have happened," she stated indignantly, as she pulled the rug firmly around her, "how many times have I had to remind you, that cleanliness is next to godliness?"

At that moment I couldn't care less what was next to godliness, all I wanted to do was get home safely and get out of the car!

As my son unloaded the shopping there was no sign of the intruder. Locking the car I vowed not to drive it again until he was located.

Following the coldest night on record, I awoke next morning to a heavy, freezing frost, and feeling sorry for my intruder of the day before, I decided to give him a fair chance to exit. Gingerly unlocking the boot I stood to one side expecting him to dart out and scurry away, not so. The sight before me almost made me sad. There lay "Mr. Jingles", curled into a tiny ball, his eyes closed, his fur stiff with frost, dead as the proverbial Dodo.

As I gingerly caught him by his stiff tail and laid him to rest under the hedge, I thought, how could I begrudge this tiny little creature that could fit into the palm of my hand, shelter in the warmth of my car, on the coldest night of the year?

Home Improvements

Marion held the tray up high. Every inch of her good tray, as she liked to call it, had to gleam tonight. After close inspection, it seemed, it would pass the test. There were other items on her checklist, no less important, that also needed to be attended to. The roast beef and pickle sandwiches, an old family favourite, rested temporarily on the kitchen counter. Later on, they would have pride of place on the French polished coffee table, in the sitting room, along with the freshly baked apple tart.

She placed some Colombian coffee, medium strength, into the percolator and switched it on. She had read somewhere in a magazine that one of the tricks of the trade, when house selling, was to greet the prospective buyers with the rich aroma of freshly brewed coffee, as they came through the door. It subconsciously made the buyer want to sign on the dotted line, apparently, though it wasn't a house that she wanted to sell tonight, but a home. She had promised her son Michael that she would really make an effort this evening.

In the background the coffee, as it brewed, made a gurgling sound. She stood in the empty kitchen, and looked out on the mature garden. The sunlight dancing off the window and the gurgling coffee had such a hypnotic effect on her that gradually, her two favourite garden shrubs, took on the shape of her husband and eight year old son, Michael, kicking a ball around on the lawn.

They laughed and tousled each other's hair and did all the rough stuff that father and sons do. Michael made an awkward pass and grimaced, as though in pain. He made for the garden bench, and his dad, with a concerned look on his face, lifted Michael's foot onto his knee and examined it as carefully as if it were the most delicate of ornaments, one that with the slightest pressure might shatter into a thousand tiny pieces. Some words were exchanged between them and Michael nodded his head in an affirmative. The hair tousling and horse play began again.

A final spurt and splutter from the percolator brought her out of her reverie and she turned from the window with slightly moist eyes. The coffee pot was full. Reaching into the cupboard for the China cups to go on the tray, she thought how proud James would have been, if he had lived to see what a fine young man their son had become.

Michael was all she had in the world now, since his father died of a heart attack twenty-two years ago. At thirty two, Michael still had his boyish good lucks and thick dark curls. He had his dad's steel blues eyes. He was now successfully running his own Landscaping business and was soon to marry a wonderful girl, Julie, whom he had met four years ago.

She wished they would get a move on, where were they, the time on the kitchen clock showed four-thirty. Mrs Roche would arrive before then if they didn't come soon. That would be a nightmare, as Mrs Roche's reputation preceded her. The way Michael had spoken about her over the years, she thought the woman arriving tonight, would be a cross between Margaret Thatcher and Hyacinth Bucket.

When he first had the pleasure of making her acquaintance, he thought she was quite a formidable woman, and it wasn't until about his fifth date with Julie, that he realised the Roche bark was apparently worse than its bite. Better mind the P's and Q's, all the same.

When everything was in place she ran upstairs to put on a dress and a new pair of tights. Surveying herself in the mirror she decided she'd go with the pearl earrings Michael and Julie had given her two Christmases ago. A nice touch she thought, considering the night that was in it.

Just as she had secured the back of the earring, she heard the unholy racket of Michael's motorbike coming up the drive. She had begged him time and time again to give up riding the infernal thing, but her pleas had been ignored. Already having lost one man in her life, she didn't want to lose another. What's more, he had Julie riding pillion on the God forsaken thing. It was hard to imagine how Julie had managed to get that one past her mother, considering the type of woman "the Rottweiler", as Michael like to call her, supposedly was.

Taking a last quick glance at herself in the mirror Marion thought that she actually didn't scrub up too badly for an "oul one". Her hair, though now turning grey at the temples, still had a lustre to it that hadn't dulled much since her young days. Her figure was still basically good even with the slight slackening of her stomach muscles. She wouldn't disgrace herself in any case.

As she reached the front door, Michael and Julie had already let themselves in, but lingered there before closing it. "Don't tell me you've even polished the door knocker mum." Michael said mischievously.

"You know, you're still not too old for a clip round the ear Mike," she replied with mock severity. "Hello, Julie love, you're looking lovely as always."

"Thanks Marion," Julie released her long auburn hair from under her helmet. "The place is looking great," she said a smile lighting her features as she glanced around. "Mum should be here soon; in fact she'll probably show up early. She always likes to make a good impression. "Isn't that right Mike?" She beamed, with a wink in his direction.

The house did look presentable for the most part. Marion was never one for standing on ceremony. She had always been a "take me as you find me type".

But she couldn't stop the butterflies from fluttering frantically in her stomach, no matter how hard she tried. Inhaling deeply, she tried to ease the tension out of her body on the exhalation that followed. As she repeated it again, and inhaled a third time for good measure, she heard the sound of tyres jarring to a halt on the gravel path, in front of the house.

Patting down her dress in an effort to smooth out some non-existent creases she felt the hem cling slightly to her leg. Looking down to fix it in place, she was horrified to find a medium sized ladder in her tights just above the knee. She tried hooshing them up slightly higher to hopefully conceal the gaping hole, when the doorbell buzzed suddenly and forced her to abandon her efforts.

Michael went to open the door and Marion stood behind him in expectation. She hoped the look of surprise did not show as standing before her on the porch was a woman who differed completely to that which she had imagined. In her mind's eye, Julie's mother was a tall, imposing woman, who carried a stern expression. But the person who stood on the threshold of her house was small and thin, with a delicate face. She fought the urge to look out further into the garden, just in case this wasn't actually Julie's mother but, maybe another unexpected guest. Her uncertainty vanished in an instant as Julie made the introductions.

"Marion, this is my mum. Mum, this is Marion." An awkward silence followed as Marion waited for this slight little woman to say what her first name was, but this never came.

"Eh, eh, Mrs Roche please come in. It's so nice to finally meet you. Here, let me take your jacket." She couldn't help noticing the mahogany colour of Mrs Roche's arms as she took the jacket and hung it on the stairs. Not necessarily an attractive look, more the appearance of a person who had been on one too many sun holidays over the years.

The sun had taken its toll and left a leathery appearance on her skin. She certainly had no shortage of money as she went for at least two foreign holidays a year, Michael had said. More than I can do, Marion thought, as she looked at Mrs Roche's stern face, I'm lucky to get a day by the seaside.

She pasted the smile that she had practised in front of the mirror, for the last week, onto her face and took her visitor into the sitting room. God, this is going to be a long, excruciating night, she thought, as Michael went to the kitchen to get the tray.

Marion led Mrs Roche over to the window and the two seater couch, she had the best view of the garden from there and it really was impressive. Her visitor sat down gingerly in the armchair, and as she did so, a pungent floral smell wafted on the air. For a woman with money to burn, you'd think she'd have better taste in perfume, Marian mused.

"I hope you were able to find the place alright," Marion offered, "Michael's directions were accurate, I hope?"

"Well, the taxi driver didn't have a problem with them," Mrs Roche returned.

"Oh, you came in a taxi?"

"Yes I've given up driving the Audi, since most of the driving I did involve travelling to and from the golf club."

"I see. You don't play golf anymore?"

"Not since my back problems started. I find it difficult now standing for long periods."

Just as Marion was about to enquire to which golf club her guest belonged, Michael arrived with the tray. As he set it down on the table Marion was none too pleased to see that there were a significantly less number of sandwiches on the plate than she remembered preparing earlier.

"Michael!" She exclaimed, angling her head towards the sandwich plate. Have you been working your way through those sandwiches behind my back?"

"Sorry mum, I was just ravenous when I came in. I couldn't help myself." He replied contritely.

"No harm done, I suppose. He was always like that growing up, Mrs Roche; hand permanently in the biscuit jar. Now, would you like tea or coffee?"

"Would you have green tea by any chance? Dr Carmody in the Beachwood clinic recommends it for my blood pressure." Her diminutive guest returned.

Marion felt the colour in cheeks heightening. "Oh, I'm awfully sorry but we're all out of green tea. Julie you didn't tell me your mother drank green tea, I could have got some specially."

"Oh there's no need, Marion," Julie said, head bowed in embarrassment. "Ordinary tea will be just fine, won't it mum?"

"Yes, I daresay it won't kill me, ordinary tea will be fine."

Michael began to pour the tea for his future mother in law, while Marion offered around the sandwiches.

When Mrs Roche reached for one, Marian detected a slight hesitation before she picked it up and examined it carefully. Dr Carmody has probably warned her off beef as well, she thought.

Well to hell with her, if she doesn't like my sandwiches, she'll probably like this even less, Marion considered, with a hint of devilment, as she fumbled on the underside of the coffee table and brought out the family photo album.

Michael's protestations fell on deaf ears as she opened the front cover, now a little frayed with time. Moving over to sit beside her guest who was growing more and more uncomfortable by the minute, Marion turned each page with care and gave a running commentary on every one. There were pictures of her and James on their wedding day. A few pictures of a holiday they took in Spain before Michael came along. Another one of Michael on his second birthday, sitting in his high chair with chocolate cake smeared all over his face.

Although the object of this photo exhibition was to have a bit of fun with Mrs Roche and make her squirm, Marion felt a lump rising in her throat. She hadn't looked at these memories for a long time and seeing James staring back at her on the happiest day of their lives was almost too much for her to bear.

Not wishing to draw attention to herself, Marion rose from her seat and began refilling tea into cups. After a few sips Mrs Roche excused herself and asked to be directed to the bathroom.

"Well this isn't going too badly." Marion said in Julie's direction.

"Oh come on Marion, It's a bloody disaster, I don't know why mum can't just lighten up a bit."

"I'm sure she's just a bit nervous, Julie love," replied Marion, not a bit convinced by her own statement. She really hadn't met such an uptight person in a long time. Maybe if she had put a few drops of whiskey into Mrs R's tea, she might have loosened up a bit, or maybe not. A whole vat of the stuff probably wouldn't have done the trick.

Marion tried over the next five minutes to convince her future daughter in law, that everything would be alright, and not to worry about her mother's visit. She told Julie that she was not in the least bit offended by her mother's odd behaviour, that in fact it had altogether been quite an entertaining evening. "Now go over and put on some music there Julie, and let's lighten the mood a bit. Nothing too racy mind you, we don't want to get your mother too excited," she said playfully.

It was only after uttering this, that she began thinking that her guest had been a little too long in the bathroom.

"I hope your mum's alright; she's been in there quite a while. Maybe I should go and check."

Marion walked across the hall to the bathroom but resisted putting her ear against the door, thinking it was just a tad unseemly, to do such a thing. Knocking softly on the door she enquired if Mrs Roche was ok. No answer came. She knocked again a little more forcefully."Mrs Roche is everything ok," she asked.

She thought she detected a slight sniffling sound from within. A few seconds more and still no answer. She had started back towards the sitting room when she heard the toilet flushing followed by the sound of a key turning. The moment Mrs Roche walked out Marion instinctively knew that something wasn't right. Her guest's eyes seemed over bright and red rimmed as if she'd had an episode of crying.

Michael strode across the hall like a man on a mission, but stopped in his tracks when Marion gave him a "leave this to me" kind of look.

"Michael, Alzheimer's is definitely setting in; I've forgotten the cream for the apple tart. Maybe you and Julie could nip round to the shop on the bike, and pick some up for me?"

The conspiratorial look that followed left him in no doubt that this was the right course of action.

As the bike rumbled out of the driveway, Marion led her guest, who was looking frailer by the minute, into the kitchen and pointed her towards a chair. Fumbling at the back of the cupboard she brought out a bottle of amber coloured liquid then poured a measure into a glass. "There you go, get that into you, and I don't care what Dr Carmody says."

To her surprise the offer was gratefully accepted. She had hardly handed it over when it was gone. Perhaps some Dutch courage had been administered along with it, as Mrs Roche finally spoke. "I'm frightfully embarrassed, please forgive me."

Marion gave her a kind look that suggested no forgiveness was necessary.

"The truth is, when you brought out those photo's I was overcome. You have such a lovely home and garden, and your son is an absolute credit to you."

"Thank you," Marion smiled back.

"It just brought home to me what a lie I've been living all these years. As you know my husband also died a while back. The children idolized him. I couldn't ever bring myself to tell them the truth."

"The truth?" Said Marion uneasily.

"The fact is that for about six years before he died he was having an affair with the wife of one of his "golfing buddies". Oh, it was an open secret between us. Quite honestly, I enjoyed the lavish lifestyle that came with being married to him. I didn't want to give that up. Despite what everyone thinks of me, I love my children and I never wanted to see them hurt either."

Marion filled her visitor's glass again, and one for herself. As the warmth of the amber liquid hit the back of her throat she couldn't help but smile at the bizarre turn this afternoon had taken.

"Will you tell your kids someday?" She asked.

"I will, one day, but certainly not right now. With the wedding coming up, that would be the cruellest thing I could ever do."

Marion reached across the table and put her hand on top of the frail woman's sitting opposite her.

Julie's mother's delicate featured face opened up into a lovely smile, the first one Marion had seen that day"One other thing, Marion, would you for God's sake call me Alice."

With that Marion began to laugh and Alice joined in with the most unburdened emotion, she had shown in years.

When the Kids start Singing

Brian stood at the bedroom window, his hot face pressed against the chill of the glass, as he stared into the night. He was vaguely aware of the bright, glittering stars that twinkled like the lights on the Christmas tree, and the frost that whitened the trees and turned the grass into icy spikes.

Why did he come back? He wondered. Does he really mean what he says? Gripping the windowsill tightly he drew a long, shuddering breath.

They were downstairs in the lounge now, together on the sofa, her head resting in the crook of his neck, listening to their favourite songs, while the light from the open fire played with the shadows in the room, and the Christmas decorations sparkled and shimmered.

He took another deep breath and pushed it past the heavy weight that had settled on his chest a year ago this very night. He still expected to hear voices raised in argument, the bang of the front door, and then the awful silence that muted all sounds and filled the house with a tension that was hard to bear.

During their rows Brian had moved through the house like a bent shadow, ignored by them both as he tiptoed around the situation.

His Gran was in a state of shock, she still hadn't recovered from his mother's announcement. They'd been having coffee at the kitchen table when she told her what she was going to do. "Are you mad, Laura?" His Gran had asked eyes wide with disbelief. "After all you've been through. After all the boys have been through, you're taking him back? It won't work, Laura, take my word for it."

"Mum please, it's for the best." His mother had pleaded. "You've got to support me in this."

"I don't know." Gran had stirred her coffee with frantic movements, sending the swirling liquid out over the rim of her cup. "What guarantees have you that he won't flit off with some ,,young one' again? And what about the effect it will have on the boys?"

"It will work," his mother had insisted, "I tell you he's changed. You've got to give him a chance for all our sakes."

That was six weeks ago, six long weeks of waiting, afraid to open his heart.

The stillness of the night seeped through the windowpane and held him as he listened to the sounds within the house.

'*I wish it could be Christmas every day.*' The words of the song drifted up from below and his mother laughed happily at something his Dad said.

In the bedroom next door his brother Tom took up the refrain, *'when the kids start singing and the band begins to play,'* shouting it out tunelessly.

In spite of himself, Brian smiled. "He hasn't a note in his head," he told the glittering stars. Tom was happy again, and Brian was glad for his younger brother, he deserved to be happy. Next minute Tom's door crashed open and his feet thumped the whole way downstairs into the sitting room.

"Are you not in bed yet?" His Dad's voice rose through the floorboards. "Here, get in there to the heat. You're frozen."

He imagined Tom's happy grin as he slid between the two of them, safe and secure, the nightmare of last Christmas forgotten. Tom was singing again in his tuneless way, *'rocking around the Christmas tree,'* his Dad was laughing at him.

How can he laugh, Brian wondered, after what he put us through?

Gran had taken charge of the situation. She had propped mum up and made the Christmas dinner that nobody ate.

"How could he do it Laura?" She had asked, shaking her head sadly as she carved the turkey. "How could he leave his family on Christmas Eve?"

"I want daddy to come home," Tom had cried, "Make him come home, mum."

Brian couldn't bear to see the pain in his mother's eyes as she tried to explain to Tom that his father wasn't coming home.

As the days passed the house became dull and cheerless. Decorations slumped like forgotten garlands. Balloons deflated into crinkled lumps. Pine needles piled high under a decrepit Christmas tree. Spiders' webs decorated every nook and cranny.

His mother seemed unaware of her surroundings. She had retreated inside herself; to some place he couldn't reach.

Brian did what he could; Gran showed him how to cook beans on toast, scrambled eggs and other simple dishes. He tidied the house, did the shopping and hid the beer cans and empty bottles from his Gran. At night when he heard his mother crying he went downstairs and made her tea. He moved Tom into his bedroom and chased his nightmares away when she was too drunk to notice. His last thought each night was for his father and the "young one" Gran said he'd gone off with, and he hated him for all the pain he had caused.

In the New Year his mother emerged, tenuous as the first sign of spring. With Gran's prompting she embarked on a course of yoga at the local community hall and changed the colour and style of her hair. With each passing week her confidence grew and their life developed a pattern once again. Then one evening in February, his father knocked on the door. Brian stayed in his room and listened to his parent's voices, his pleading, hers crying.

According to Gran the "young one" had upped and left his father a couple of weeks after they got together.

"That's young ones for you," she told Brian, "they break up a marriage and then drop the man like a hot potato. And it served him right for going with her in the first place."

He called again and again, as the summer wore on. He wanted his family back. Brian watched him come and go from his bedroom window, watched Tom run to meet him like an excited puppy, saw his mother's face light up when he smiled at her, and heard the disappointment in his father's voice when he wouldn't come down to see him.

"You may wait until he's ready," his mother had said, "give him time."

"Bedtime," he heard his mother say to Tom, "it's nearly twelve o'clock."

"Ah mum," Tom groaned.

"C'mon," said his father, "I'll see you up."

'Silent night, holy night,' the choir surged through the floor and filled his room with sound. There was a tap on his door, then his mother's voice, "can I come in Brian?"

'All is calm, all is bright,' sang the choir.

His mother joined him at the window. "What a sky," she said, "it's beautiful." But Brian wasn't looking at the sky; he was watching his mother's face, and the glow that radiated from it, brighter than the glittering stars.

With a tender smile she put her arm around his shoulders and hugged him to her.

'Round the virgin mother and child, holy infant so tender and mild.'

"Happy Christmas Brian," she kissed him softly on the cheek, "we're going to have a great Christmas this year, Brian, a great Christmas." Behind the sureness in her voice there was also a plea, a silent plea from her to him

"Promise?" asked Brian as he leaned into the warmth of her embrace.

"With all my heart," she answered fervently as the door opened again.

"Can I come in son?" It was a tentative request from his father as he hesitated in the doorway.

Brian turned towards the door and for the first time in nearly a year met his father's eyes, those eyes full of uncertainty as they searched his.

"Sure Dad," he said as the choir sang, *'Sleep in heavenly peace. Sleep in heavenly peace.'*

Slowly, his father entered the room his steps hesitant and unsure, his eyes intent on Brian's face.

"Happy Christmas son," he whispered as he laid a faltering hand on Brian's shoulder.

Brian saw the love in his father's eyes and a surge of happiness entered his heart as slowly, ever so slowly, the heavy weight on his chest disappeared and he was filled with the stillness and majesty of the night.

R.S.V.P

Dear Melissa,

Thank you so much for the invitation to Erica's wedding. I was absolutely thrilled to receive it. I had heard some time ago about her engagement to Stephen, so I must admit I was expecting to hear from you. Is that the young man I met her with when she came over on holidays and visited us in Cork?

I was really embarrassed on that occasion, as I did not realise that he was not of our persuasion, when I asked him if he attended Sunday Mass. However we glossed over it and had an enjoyable afternoon tea. He seemed very nice and so handsome, and very eligible too, by all accounts. His sports car caused quite a stir in the village.

I have selected a very fashionable outfit, in a deep shade of cerise, for the wedding reception. It was a special in the Sue Ryder shop. The local dressmaker is making an off the shoulder dress for me, from some old curtains that I had in my flat before I moved to the sheltered accommodation, this I will wear to the night before dinner. I am in a quandary though about whether I should wear the hat I bought at the local jumble sale, in aid of the Christmas Appeal Fund. I believe it's made by someone called, Philip Tracey, but I never met anyone of that name staying in our sheltered accommodation.

I like it so much, I have decided to wear it at the 'over seventies' morning, we have them every week. It might be a little bit over the top for the wedding though, I know that people of the 'other persuasion' can be a bit conservative, and I wouldn't want to let the side down. The hat is a deep shade of purple with a plume of ostrich feathers, that nod and bob as I teeter along in my Jimmy Choo high heels, those I bought at the local Sunday Car Booth Sale. The only problem is, the shoes are a size too big and I am afraid I might trip and stumble when walking down the aisle in the church, as they're quite high, higher than I'm used to wearing. But if my bunions start acting up with the bad weather, I need the extra size. I'll decide about wearing the hat nearer to the wedding.

I hope you are keeping well, and the rest of the family. I am looking forward to seeing you all. I have just one request, could you arrange to have my food liquidised as my false teeth are inclined to fall out if I chew my food too quickly?

I know I should get new ones fitted as my gums have shrunk over the years, and the 'dentafix' doesn't hold them in place any longer, but seeing as I only wear them now on special occasions, like Mass on a Sunday, I'm not too bothered. Anyway the good news is I'm on a three month waiting list for new dentures.

One more thing I forgot to mention, when you are arranging the place settings, don't put me near any electrical equipment as my hearing aid will start to whistle, and don't sit me near cousin Anita, don't forget we haven't spoken in fifty years, and I have no intention of wasting my breath on her again.

After all, why should I forgive her? She took the money from the till in Grandma's shop all those years ago, and put the blame on me. She was believed, oh yes, all she had to do was bat her eyelids and cry and the whole world would come running to her aid.

Grandma was so angry that she gave Anita all her jewellery, even though she promised me the sapphire pendant, with matching ear-rings and bracelet. I suppose she'll wear that to the wedding just to spite me, so make sure we're not sitting anywhere near one another. I wouldn't want to demean myself by tearing it off her scrawny neck, and I might do so if I get enough Sherries into me!

Anyway I'm really looking forward to seeing you all and I can't wait for the twenty third of September to come around.

Your loving great aunt,

Kate.

P.S. I forgot to mention that I will be bringing Harry, as the invitation read Melissa and Guest. He is my constant companion these days and I couldn't leave him behind as he will sulk and I won't get any good of him for days after.

The only problem is that he is inclined to snore. I hope he doesn't fall asleep during the ceremony I've just remembered something; he hates dogs, especially poodles, so I hope nobody brings one. I'll put a muzzle on him, as they say that German shepherds can snap when in a crowd. He's the dog I rescued from the dog pound some time ago, but don't worry, he'll rest at my feet in the church so there shouldn't be a problem, unless he falls asleep during the ceremony. I wouldn't like his snoring to be heard above the wedding music.

As always,

Kate

Super-size me

Tom checked his watch as he drained the last mouthful of coffee from his mug. Four thirty, time to check the cells again. He didn't mind the night shift; it was usually very quiet, which suited him. He glanced at the small blonde woman reading a magazine at the other table. "Time to move Kate, cell watch, we should get going."

Kate stood up and stretched her limbs. "I don't know why we bother, nothing much is going to happen, this lot's very quiet."

"Rules are rules," Tom replied, "let's go." Out in the dimly lit corridor, Tom started checking the doors on the left, Kate, those on the right. They walked along in silence, their rubber soled shoes squeaking on the polished floor as they lifted the flap on each door, and checked on the condition of the inmates. As Kate neared the last cell on the corridor, she could hear something, like a faint knocking sound.

Cell nineteen. Carol Somers cell, automatically Kate recalled Carol's report sheet. Homeless, petty thief, drug addiction, harmless enough, hadn't given any trouble since she arrived a week ago, probably having a nightmare. She lifted the flap and looked inside "Oh Jesus," horrified, she reeled back and screamed, "Tom the keys, quick, it's a suicide attempt!"

"Carol wake up, Carol can you hear me!" Kate cried. They cut her down and lay her on the bunk bed. Immediately Tom tried to resuscitate her as Kate called for help

"It's no good, Kate, she's gone." Tom sighed deeply; this was the second suicide attempt he'd had in his thirty years as a prison officer, and his second failure at resuscitation. He knew that weeks from now he would still be asking himself why he didn't spot the signs, but then the quiet ones were always hard to read.

He stood up, and then gently pulled the sheet over Carol's body. As he did so, a folded sheet of paper fell to the floor. "Kate, I think Carol's left a note," He retrieved the paper and began to read.

"I'm not addressing this letter to any one in particular because I don't have anybody left; my vanity drove away all the people who once were in my life; my children, my husband the only man who ever loved me, and all my friends.

I used to be a plump woman, I was some pounds overweight, nothing much, I think now. But for me it was like a tonne. I was very conscious of my weight and became obsessed with that. I joined all the programmes, I did every single diet that came across my path, the tea diet, the ice cream one, the peanut butter one, the milk shake for breakfast, Atkins diet, etcetera. But I had bad eating habits and my lack of discipline and consistency never allowed me to succeed.

I was also a member of a gym, every morning I spent at the pool. I used to enjoy the chat with the other women at the Jacuzzi and the coffee afterwards, but somehow during the conversation the topic of weight was always in the air. It was on one of those mornings, that I met the woman who would change my life forever.

Jane was introduced to me, as Sheila's friend. She was extremely good looking, with a mane of long blond hair tied up in a ponytail, her clothes appeared to be very expensive and very trendy, and, she had a body to die for. When we went for coffee she sat down next to me and I was very surprised to see her ordering a large, full fat cappuccino, with sugar and a portion of chocolate cake with cream on the side, which she devoured in an instant.

Jokingly, I asked for the secret; but well I knew, she probably was going to starve herself for the rest of the day. It was then she told me that once, she was fat, but now, she was losing weight without being on a diet or doing exercise.

"Wow, what are you using?" I asked, "I have to get my hands on that."

"The tablets are a little bit expensive but it's worth it," she confided, "the results are amazing, as you can see."

Jane said she could supply me with the tablets as she was an agent for the company. I followed her out to the car park and over to her Mercedes. The boot was full of boxes containing slimming pills. I got two weeks treatment from her and started taking the tablets the following morning. At the end of the first week I was a stone lighter, by week two I had lost over two stone in weight. I was feeling fantastic, very energetic, my skin was glowing and my hair shining, and I was eating everything I wanted. I wasn't depriving myself, life couldn't be better.

The day I finished the last tablet I phoned Jane. I wanted two more weeks of treatment, another two stone was all I needed to lose, but this time the tablets were more expensive and I could only get a week's supply. It was worth it, I thought, so I paid up and continued losing weight. My friends and family told me I was looking fantastic, everyone was noticing me; even strangers were giving me appreciative glances. My husband, Peter, was looking at me differently, I was a desirable woman again, I felt confident and attractive, and for the first time in years I was able to go to the shops and buy clothes I only wore in my dreams.

When I went to get the dosage for the next week I was told that the tablets were now five times more expensive than the week before, I had with me the money to pay for my daughter's piano lessons and used it to get the tablets. I lied to my husband and told him the piano classes were cancelled. That was the first lie, after that lying became second nature to me.

The following week I had decided that I had reached my ideal weight, I looked better than I had in years and I didn't need any more tablets. Jane rang inquiring if I needed tablets for the week. "I'm not taking anymore, Jane, I've lost enough weight so I don't need them now." Anyway I thought they're too expensive and I couldn't afford them.

Two days later I rang Jane, pleading for more tablets. I had put back on six pounds. She brought them over immediately and as I closed the door behind her I realised I was going to be taking them for ever.

In only a few weeks all the money we had for the children's college education was gone, when that finished I started taking money from the bank account. I tried to hide the statements when they arrived in the post. It was only a matter of time before Peter found out. When he confronted me I couldn't say anything, I didn't know how to explain myself.

He was furious and demanded my bank cards, which he cut in two. He wouldn't let me have access to any money in the bank so I started selling things, first my jewellery and after that, bits and pieces belonging to the household.

Peter was getting very suspicious and tried very hard to get the truth out of me, but I couldn't make myself tell him what was going on. He didn't trust me anymore I wasn't allowed to have access to any money. He was filling the car with petrol and buying groceries and all the things needed at home. Our relationship faded away, we weren't talking at all, I was afraid of a confrontation.

When I wasn't able to get any money, I went to see Jane and explained my problem. She suggested prostitution, but I couldn't do that. At that stage I couldn't bear to live without the tablets I needed them. I tried several times to give them up, but weight wasn't the problem anymore, my body was so used to them I just couldn't function if I didn't take them.

I was desperate; I needed money and found shoplifting a good way to get it. After only a few weeks I got very confident but my luck changed, I was caught. The police called Peter, he was very embarrassed. Afterwards at home, in the privacy of our bedroom, he demanded an explanation to my behaviour.

When I wouldn't tell him he asked me to leave the house and avoid any contact with the children, because I wasn't fit enough to be a mother.

I packed my things, and left without even saying goodbye to the children, my eyes were covered in tears. I turned to see Peter's face and his cold stare was the last memory I had of him.

I was living in the car; I didn't have the courage to ask anyone else for a place to stay. I couldn't move the car because I needed to choose between money for petrol and money for tablets. I found a good parking space where I was able to leave the car all day and night.

To survive I started stealing from supermarkets and chain stores. Any clothes I stole I managed to sell on the back streets. As long as I had enough to buy the tablets that's all that mattered. My life was miserable, I missed the children and my home but somehow, the tablets made me able to endure every day.

I was brought to the police station by a security man from a supermarket; he had been keeping an eye on me and was able to make a very strong case. The public defender couldn't do anything for me. I was sentenced to two years, probably less if I behaved properly, but I'm not able to survive without my medicine. I destroyed my life because I wanted to look beautiful and became a horrible person trying to succeed. I can't live like this, tell Peter I'm sorry."

Wearily, Tom walked out into the morning sunshine, he felt exhausted, but he couldn't go home yet, anyway he wouldn't sleep. The night had passed in a daze for him and Kate; they had shuffled through their shift on automatic pilot. He'd grab a cup of coffee from the all-night cafe and sit in the park while he sorted out in his mind what to do. The park was empty except for the occasional jogger.

Sitting on a bench he sipped his coffee slowly. He thought of his wife, Jane, and the great job she had landed six months ago, working for a pharmaceutical company based in America. The money was great, granted she worked hard, on call at all hours, but the perks were brilliant, and that Mercedes she had? It was some company car!

"Well, not for long more, she'd have to give it all up now," he reasoned. "She'd see the sense in that."

He put his hand in his pocket and pulled out a bottle of slimming tablets.

"Thank God I hadn't started taking them, he thought," I'd rather have this beer belly on me than end up like poor Carol!"

Ellen and the Vet

Ellen looked out the window at the stray cats. A collection of skin and bones really. She felt sorry for them, but living on her own meant she hadn't that many scraps and she wasn't going to buy food for them. Time for a visit to the vet, he'd sort it out for her, besides she liked talking to that young man – such a gentleman. On her way out she smiled at her reflection in the hall mirror, "you don't look a day over forty," she told herself.

In the surgery John Dowling was having his own problems. His assistant had to go to a funeral and Jill his receptionist had rang in sick. He was on the phone when Ellen Magee walked in.

"Good morning John," she called out.

"Ah Mrs Magee," he said, one hand over the phone, "I'll be with you in a minute."

"Please don't rush on my account John," she said, giving her hair the inevitable pat. She walked to a seat with measured steps. Well she did have her stilettos on. They were old she knew, but they gave ones legs such a good shape.

"Now Mrs Magee, what can I do for you? I'm afraid that if it isn't an emergency I'll have to attend to it some other time." This was a woman that could go on for hours and he was hoping that today wasn't the day. Cutting across her before she could say a word he said that he was short-staffed and would have to close the surgery for the morning.

"Now John, don't you dare do that, I can help you. What would I have to do?"

Thoughts were racing through his head. Could she do it? It really would be just answering the phone. Even as he was thinking about it he was grabbing up his case and heading for the door. "Thanks Mrs Magee."

"Please call me Ellen," she said primly.

"Right so Ellen, just answer the phone and explain to anyone who calls that if it's an absolute emergency I can be reached on my mobile. The number is on the desk. Thanks Ellen."

The hair was again patted into shape as she stepped behind the counter. "Such a mess," she said, talking to herself and looking around, how could anyone work here? Poor John, she decided, hadn't very good staff. Picking up pens and pencils and the phone she stopped in mid-air.

"Yes, definitely to the right, I am right-handed so it makes more sense." Standing back to admire her work she felt it looked better already. Notepad

Somewhere West of London

It's Hereford not Hertford.
Though both are west of London
An 'E' not a 'T' spells the place t'was once my home.

Wooded hills, verdant vales,
West of London, next to Wales
I travelled east and left its pastures long ago.

Coventry, home to be,
Midland city west of London.
No pastures here though pastures new I'd hoped to find.

Seventy four, Africa's shore
South and east of London.
Sunny days, busy days, pastures not an option.

Cleethorpes next, meridian
Town, north not west of London.
Good friends I made in that place beside the Humber.

Further then to Yorkshire
North and west of London
Village small, pastures wide, my home 'til I retired.

Wooded hills, verdant vales,

West of London, west of Wales;

Midland county, lovely Laois; my home until I die

From Hereford to Laois.

In Strongbow's steps I have trodden.

I was born, I will die, somewhere west of London

The House by the River

Anne rarely thought of her grandmothers, as to her loss, they played no part in her life. Hearing her friends describe theirs, in great detail set her thinking. Anne's gran, on her mother's side, died before she was born, while gran, Kate, on her father's side, lived with her only daughter, Bridie, beside the wide tidal river Suir, outside Waterford City.

Through her childhood years, her father reminisced constantly about when he was a young boy, living on the banks of the river Suir. He would talk at length about the fun he had with his friends swimming in the great river and roaming the countryside that bordered its length. When he was older, he loved nothing better than, after the day's work was finished, to ramble across the fields to the neighbouring houses for a "seisuin", until the early hours of the morning.

Anne loved to hear him talk about when he was a boy and she'd conjured up images of the house, gran Kate and auntie Bridie, but she never got to visit his birth place until she was eight years old.

She could still remember how excited she felt that morning jumping out of bed, wide awake as the sky filled with light, and running down the stairs in the still dark, silent house. Her mother's voice scolded her from behind her parent's bedroom door, with a warning to get back into bed as it was too early to be up.

Eventually, the agonisingly long morning passed and the clock said ten minutes to twelve. Anne could hardly contain herself as she buttoned her coat and then ran her comb through her hair. Aunt Bridie was to arrive at twelve and they would walk to the house in the country. Her heart jumped when the knocker banged loudly off the front door. She ran into the hall as her mother opened the door and there stood a woman so unlike the aunt she had imagined. She was tall and bony with her dark hair pulled back from her pinched face and tied into a knot. Her mouth was grim and set and she looked like she never smiled, not at all like Anne's father who was always smiling and laughing.

The journey to the house was spent mostly in silence. Bridie asked three questions of Anne; how old was she, did she help her mother in the house, and had she made her holy communion. Anne answered politely as she would a stranger for she felt no bond with her aunt and was actually slightly afraid of her. She hoped her gran Kate would turn out to be more like she had imagined.

The house was just like her father had described. It nestled into the side of a hill, down a lane bordered with sturdy beech trees. The sun glinted on the panes of its tall windows, lending a warm glow to the walls. The front lawn was edged by a flower bed, still holding remnants of summer flowers. A gravel path led from the lawn to an orchard sheltered from the wind by a hedge of laurel. As Anne followed her aunt on the little path that led around to the back of the house she gasped with delight at the sight of the river flowing like a silver ribbon between the fields.

Her aunt brought her as far as the back door of the house and pushed the door open. A dank smell rose to greet her in a dark and gloomy scullery. Under a narrow window, a grey coloured meat safe dominated a small table and a large green press stood against the far wall. Overhead, a clothesline ran the length of the wall festooned with dish cloths that had seen better days. She followed her aunt through to the kitchen.

"Wait there." Bridie pointed to a chair by the large, wooden kitchen table," I'll get your gran."She crossed the flag stone floor and went through a door, closing it smartly behind her.

Anne could heard muted voices and reckoned it must be the parlour and she imagined her gran seated in an armchair busily knitting. The door opened and an old, stooped woman, dressed all in black, her glasses perched on the end of her nose, shuffled into the kitchen with the aid of a walking stick. She stopped by the open fire and sat on the armchair there. "Come here, child," she said.

Hesitantly Anne moved towards her gran. She wasn't at all like she had imagined. Anne had picture her younger, going on her father's description of his mother. Her gran smelt of lavender and mothballs, her dark brown eyes, set in a wrinkled face, peered over the top of her glasses.

"There you are child," she said patting Anne's head as she looked closely at her. "You don't look like your father at all, do you? I suppose you must take after your mother's side of the family." With that she sat back in the chair and closed her eyes.

"Go out and play in the orchard," Bridie ordered, "I'll call you in when the tea is ready."

Annie was glad to be outside in the afternoon sun even though a cold breeze blew off the distant river. She amused herself piling fallen apples into heaps and then spelling out her name with them.

The evening was drawing in when her aunt called her. The meal of tea, bread and jam was eaten in silence. The doors were closed and locked. The Tilly lamp, which stood in the middle of the wooden table, was coaxed into light, throwing shadows into unfamiliar corners. The black stove was fuelled in anticipation of a long night. Anne sat on the edge of her chair, taking in the scene.

Aunt Birdie and gran Kate sat by the fire talking in hushed tones, occasionally they'd look in her direction, the word bed was mentioned.

Bed, what did they mean? Panic set in, as did Anne's determination to spend the night in her own cosy bed. She soon gave voice to that determination.

Extensive promises and coaxing from both her aunt Bridie and gran Kate fell on deaf ears. Anne was near to tears when eventually aunt Bridie gave in and told her to put her coat on. Tears turned to relief as Anne quickly buttoned her coat. Soon they were outside the front door, facing the cold dark night. With the aid of a torch they took the homeward bound road.

Few words passed between them as they hurried along, the only sound was the click-clack of their steps in contrast to the gentle lapping of the river Suir.

To Anne as an eight year old, who wasn't used to being out after dark, every sound she heard from the bushes was the cry of the banshee, and she was positive they would meet the Headless Horseman somewhere on the journey home.

After what seemed like an endless walk, Anne sighed with relief as the twinkling lights of Waterford City appeared where she was delivered safely to the bosom of her family.

A disgruntled aunt Bridie had a quick cup of tea and then her none too happy father had to walk his sister back down the country road to the house by the river.

He had no way of knowing, but it would be his last visit to his old home, as gran Kate died soon after, and Bridie surprised the family by emigrating to America.

Anne would have liked to have known both her grannies better, but she now knows, it was from her gran Kate she inherited her blood pressure, arthritis and varicose veins.

The Box

Betty takes the hairbrush from her bag. Brushing other people's hair is not something she particularly enjoys doing, especially older people. There's something about thinning hair sitting on top of a pink, blotchy scalp that made her a little queasy, but she would force herself to do it, today.

She puts the brush to her father's scalp. His hair has been thinning a lot over the years so it is a particular challenge for her not to gag, as the teeth of the brush meet the exposed skin underneath the few wisps he has left. She brushes it as quickly as she can, just enough to make him look presentable. Soon it is done. Betty looks at her handiwork, satisfied she has done a reasonable job.

Next she turns her attention to his tie. He is wearing a deep, bottle green one with little wine coloured flecks running through it. She straightens it out and smoothes it down. Stepping back Betty surveys her ministrations, not that her dad would appreciate it of course. He let himself go to the dogs over the last few years, after her mum went.

Well not to worry, he will be looking his best today for all the family, in his finest bib and tucker. We can all keep the pretence up that everything is ok, and sing his praises. It's what he has always loved to hear. Nobody ever dared say otherwise. They wouldn't get what they were due then.

One had to look at the bigger picture; they need only play the dutiful daughters and sons for a few more days. They had practised their parts well. What was coming to them all was payment enough after the way he treated their mum. The wait will be worth it.

She shouldn't be hypocritical, she supposed, isn't that why I'm standing here running a brush over his mangy head, she mused.

"Well, daddy, say goodbye to your precious house. You always said the only way you would ever leave here was in a box. Well, you get your wish today, you miserable old sod."

Betty looks down at the elaborate coffin, fit for a man of his means, and bends to kiss his waxen face one last time, but she couldn't. There were other preparations to be made before the vultures descended to say their final goodbyes.

Ghosts in the Attic

"Annie! Annie come here, I want you." The petulant voice carried down the stairs into the quiet kitchen, where the children sat engrossed in their homework, at the big wooden table. As one they turned to look at their mother, who was busy ironing by the window, her face strained and flushed from her efforts.

"Annie, come here at once." The petulant voice insisted.

With a loud sigh Annie upended the iron and banged it down on the windowsill. "That woman will be the death of me," she muttered as she wiped perspiration from her face with the end of her apron. Slowly she turned away from the table, her hand pressed into the small of her back as she gingerly arched her spine.

"Will I go up for you, Mam?" In an instant Angela was on her feet, her chair scraping the tiled floor as she pushed away from the table. She closed her copy and made a neat pile of her books, "Will I Mam?" She jiggled her hips, restless as a long legged filly, her hand on the hall door ready for flight.

"Oh thanks, love." A smile spread across Annie's features lighting her eyes and relieving the lines of tension on her face. "She probably wants a cup of tea. I'll put the kettle on."

"Ah that's not fair," Cathy moaned. "She always gets to go. Mam, that's not fair."

"Would you shut up whinging?" Seamus scowled at Cathy from under his black eyebrows.

Angela hesitated in the doorway, glanced at Cathy, then at her mother.

"Go on Angela." Annie said firmly as she manoeuvred her way across the kitchen to the black range.

"It's just not fair," Cathy pulled a sulky face at Annie. "She always gets to go."

"It's just not fair," mimicked Seamus. "Mam, would you tell her to stop?" Exasperated, he ran his fingers through his wiry hair. "I can't do me sums with listening to her."

"Hush now the pair of you."

"But Mam," Cathy wailed.

"Maybe next time, Cathy." Annie bent over the range and pulled the large, black kettle onto the hob. Instantly, it started singing.

"Really?" Cathy enquired.

Annie ignored her youngest daughter. "Are you having trouble with those sums, Seamus?"

"No," he growled. "Just tell her to shut up."

"Do you really mean it Mam, really?" Cathy persisted.

"Yes. Now drop it Cathy, like a good girl."

Cathy beamed with delight. "Thanks Mam."

"Satisfied now?" Seamus asked his voice full of sarcasm.

Cathy glanced quickly at her mother's back, then turned to Seamus and stuck her tongue out as far as she could.

"Mam, did you see what she did, Mam?"

"That's enough of that now. Enough!" There was an edge to Annie's voice as she eyed the pair of them across the table. "Get on with your homework," she told their watchful faces as she took the tea caddy from the press by the fire.

With a smug look at Seamus, Cathy bent to her homework.

Liam, who had been colouring a picture in his copybook, put down the crayon he was using. "Hey, Mam," he ventured, "why is Granny so cross?"

"Oh God!" Groaned Seamus, "because she's old and sick, that's why."

"Seamus! That's enough." Annie warned.

"Is that right Mam?" Liam looked to her for confirmation.

"She's not cross all the time, pet," Annie indulged her youngest with an affectionate smile, "only when she's sick, like any of us."

"Am I cross when I get sick?" He asked his brown eyes solemn.

Seamus snorted. "God Ma, will you tell him to shut up? I can't do me sums with him. You're stupid, Liam," he said, wrinkling his nose in disgust, "a stupid little baby."

"I'm not stupid," protested Liam, as he turned on Seamus with a fierce scowl.

"Stupid baby, stupid baby." Seamus taunted.

"Mam, he said I was stupid." Liam wailed. "Mam, tell him to stop."

"Leave him alone Seamus." Cathy put her arm around her young brother. "If there's anyone stupid it's you. You can't even do your sums."

"Nobody's stupid in this house," Annie hissed, her cheeks sporting bright red spots on her pale face, "or a baby." She turned to Seamus with a warning look. "Now, if you don't behave yourself I'll tell your father when he comes in from work. Is that clear?"

Seamus glowered at her from under his eyebrows.

"Is that clear?" Her voice was low, each word distinct and separate.

"Yes." Seamus muttered under his breath.

"Good. Now get on with your homework. And you get back to your colouring, love," she said softly to Liam.

Clutching the tea caddy to her chest she stood with her back to the fire, eyeing her family as the heat of the range radiated out around her. With a soft sigh her left hand found the ache in the small of her back and her fingers kneaded deeply as her nylon blouse crackled against her pinafore. The clock ticked evenly on the mantelpiece and upstairs Gran grumbled as Angela chattered on like a cheeky sparrow.

"Is your back sore, Mam?" Cathy enquired.

"No, I was just scratching an itchy spot." She smiled distractedly and her hand fluttered to her hair, pushing a stray lock behind her ear.

Seamus glanced at her, a determined look shaping on his face, as he twirled his pencil round and round his fingers.

"What's wrong?" She enquired, "Are you stuck with a sum?"

He shook his head, his dark eyes studying her, the pencil twirling and twirling.

"What is it?" She urged. "What's the matter?"

"Where did you get us, Mam?" He asked, his voice low, his eyes glued to hers. "Where did we come from?" The words danced across the table and hung before her, shimmering in the heat.

Her face went blank and she turned quickly towards the range. "What do you mean?" She asked, as she busied herself with the teapot.

"Timmy Dunne said you laid all of us, like a hen lays eggs."

"My Mammy's not a hen," Liam declared, "you're stupid, Seamus, real stupid!"

For once Seamus ignored Liam's taunts, his eyes riveted on Annie's busy back, watching for her reaction. Full of bravado now, he puffed out his chest. "And," he continued, "When a woman is going to have a baby she gets fat. Real fat," he stressed.

Three pairs of eyes locked in on her, suddenly aware of her shapeless pinafore and loosely tied apron, as the black, shiny kettle hissed and boiled and sent clouds of steam into the atmosphere.

"Did he now." She opened the tea caddy and slowly three spoonfuls of tea found their way into the teapot. "Did he now indeed," she repeated as the boiling water followed the tea leaves. She plonked the empty kettle down at the side of the range. "Timmy Dunne would be better off sticking to his sums." Slowly she stirred the tea round and round, the spoon scraping off the teapot's sides as it did the circuit. Round and round it went into the silence as the clock ticked and the children waited, all agog.

"Well, Mammy did ya?" Seamus couldn't contain himself any longer; he strained forward on the table, his chin jutting out. "Did you, Mammy? Did you lay us?"

Before Annie could reply, Angela burst in through the kitchen door, her eyes bright with excitement. "Mam, Aunt Peggy's cycling up the laneway, and she's got a basket on the carrier," she announced breathlessly. "I saw her from Granny's window. Oh, and Granny wants cream crackers and tea, and a bit of hard cheese," she skirted around the table and opened the back door.

"Aunt Peggy's here," Liam shouted as he jumped down from his chair and ran through the door. "Come on, Cathy," he cried. She might have sweets for us."

Cathy followed eagerly. "Are you coming, Seamus?" She asked over her shoulder.

Seamus ignored her, his eyes fixed on his mother's figure.

Annie continued her stirring, her back bent over the pot until she heard Peggy's voice.

How are all the Molloys?" Peggy asked cheerfully as she swept into the kitchen, with Liam by the hand. Angela and Cathy following close behind.

"We're all fine," answered Annie as she placed the lid on the teapot, "just fine."

"I timed that well," Peggy remarked, eyeing the tea pot, as she put her basket on the table. Taking off her coat she draped it over the back of a chair.

"Auntie Peggy's got sweets for us," Liam said eagerly as he tugged at her skirt, "in her basket."

"Sweets for everyone," Peggy laughed, as she removed a brown paper bag. "Here Angela, you give them out when you've finished your homework. The same amount for everyone," she warned.

"And when you've finished your homework, you can all go out to play." Annie informed them.

"Ah Ma," Liam pleaded, "I want to stay with you and Auntie Peggy."

"For a little while maybe," Peggy gave him a quick hug. "Now go on back to the table and finish your nice picture."

"You're looking tired, Annie." There was concern in Peggy's voice, as her eyes swept over her sister's frame. "You're doing too much, as usual." She pulled the armchair over to the table. "Now sit down there," she ordered and I'll get the tea." Peggy took three cups from the press, put them on the table and reached for the teapot.

"I'll take Granny up her tea," Angela volunteered. "And she wants cheese and crackers too."

"Tell your Granny that I've lovely fresh eggs, soda bread and country butter, if she'd prefer. A present from your other Gran in the country," Peggy said, passing the cup of tea to Angela. "Now mind that cup on the stairs," she warned. "Here is yours Annie."

"Thanks Peggy." Annie took the tea and slowly sank back into the armchair.

"You'd want to be minding yourself," Peggy chided, her voice low, as she looked pointedly at Annie's stomach, "and not be running up and down those stairs at her beck and call." She took the soda bread and country butter out of the basket; "I'm surprised at Jim agreeing to take her in, especially now, when you're like this."

"There's no one else to look after her," Annie said wearily.

"What about Jim's bachelor brother?" Peggy took the large, brown bowl off the dresser and put it on the table.

"He works all hours, he's never at home. So that leaves me." Annie shrugged her shoulders, "I can manage most of the time."

"That's not good enough." Peggy stated, as with great care she unwrapped each egg from its cushion of newspaper, and then placed them gently in the bowl.

"I know." Annie sighed heavily. "Anyway, we'll talk about it later, when we're alone." She looked across the table and caught Seamus's eye.

He stared back at her unblinking.

Quickly she turned away, a flush creeping up her neck and into her face.

"Are you okay, Annie?" A puzzled look settled on Peggy's features. She turned quickly and scanned the children's faces. "What's going on?"

"Nothing,"Annie replied, "nothing at all."

"What's wrong with Seamus, then? He hasn't said a word since I came in." She studied Seamus's sullen face.

"Seamus said Mammy was a hen, and that she laid us all," Liam piped, "didn't ya Seamus?"

"I didn't say Mammy was a hen," Seamus stated, his face bright red. "That's not what I said."

"Well now, isn't that a silly story." Peggy said slowly, as she took the bowl of eggs over to the dresser, "a very silly story indeed!"

"It's not a silly story," ranted Seamus, his eyes glittering with rage. "Timmy Dunne told me, and he knows!" He sat back in his chair, folded his arms across his chest and stared defiantly at Annie.

"If you paid more attention to the schoolmaster and less to Timmy Dunne," Annie remarked as with a sudden burst of energy she eased her bulk out of the armchair, "you wouldn't be having problems with your sums." Going to the press under the sink she picked out a saucepan. "You'd want to buck up your ideas, now me lad," she warned, as she filled the pan with water, "your school work is beginning to suffer, and your father won't be pleased with that!"

"Do you want some eggs in that, Annie?" Peggy enquired softly.

"Aye," Annie answered, handing over the saucepan. "If I were you now Seamus," she advised, "I'd just concentrate on my homework. She stared at him until he lowered his head.

Peggy put the saucepan on the range, filled the black kettle and pulled it onto the hob. Then, opening the fire door she threw turf onto the glowing coals. The dry turf whooshed as it caught alight, the sound loud in the silence that had settled over the kitchen.

Upstairs in the front bedroom, the old woman's voice was a low grumble as she talked to Angela.

"Okay Gran," Angela's voice sang out as her feet sounded on the stairs. She bounded into the kitchen, shattering the stillness. "Granny would love a boiled egg and some soda bread," she announced.

Galvanised into action Annie went to the table and began slicing the soda bread. "Angela, you can go back to your homework now. Peggy would you get down the tray from the mantelpiece and we'll lay it for Granny's tea."

"Which cup is hers?" Peggy asked, "I'll get it off the dresser."

"The china cup," Annie replied, "and will you get a plate and egg cup too?"

Seamus watched from under his eyebrows as the two sisters went about their tasks, gnawing the end of his pencil until he had it chewed into a soggy lump.

Annie ignored him as she buttered the bread and placed it on the plate. "The kettle's starting to boil," Peggy reported, "and the eggs won't take long. What way does she like them, hard or soft?"

"Oh, runny and watery," Annie replied with the touch of a smile at her lips.

"Just like herself, then," Peggy said humorously.

Annie looked at her sister and laughed. "I'd better empty the teapot, and make a fresh drop."

She was just about to reach for the pot when Seamus flung his pencil across the table.

"Then what about the black bag you're hiding?" He shouted at her, "It's full of baby clothes, and your nightgown and things."

For an instant, Annie's hand hovered over the pot handle, and then she slowly turned towards him, her face white and hard as granite. "What bag is that now?" Her voice was soft as she leaned across the table.

"The bag under the stairs, in the cubby hole." He stared into her eyes, challenging her.

She met his challenge with an unwavering gaze.

Blushing to the roots of his hair, he lowered his eyes.

"Angela, would you go and look under the stairs for a black bag," she asked, never once taking her eyes off Seamus.

"What black bag, Mam?" Angela asked, bewildered.

"Just go and look, Angela. There's a good girl."

Mystified, Angela went to do her bidding.

The clock ticked time away on the mantelpiece as the door of the cubbyhole under the stairs creaked open and Angela rummaged inside. "There's no black bag in here," her muffled voice reached into the kitchen.

"Thanks Angela, you can sit down now and finish your homework." Annie straightened her posture, "did you hear that, Seamus? No black bag under the stairs. What will you be thinking of next, ghosts in the attic?"

With a mutinous glance in her direction Seamus bent to his homework, his pencil digging into the paper as he worked it across the copy.

Once again, silence descended on the kitchen as the children settled to their studies.

Annie stood watching them, her back to the fire, her hands folded over her high stomach, a smile playing at the corners of her mouth.

Peggy stood at her side, her eyes bright. "Tell me," she said softly, "where's the bag now?"

Annie turned towards her, a grin spreading across her face. "In granny's room, under the bed," she whispered.

"Thank God for that," Peggy replied, her shoulders shaking with silent mirth as she eyed Seamus's bent head, while behind them, the kettle hissed and the eggs bubbled gaily in the pan.

"Come on Peggy," Annie said with a catch in her voice, "let's get this tea organised." Then she turned her back and reached for the teapot just as the old woman's voice carried down the stairs and into the kitchen, demanding her eggs and soda bread.

Suit for a Twin

Paul was delighted to meet his twin brother again. After thirty years apart it was just the same as if it was yesterday. The same bond of friendship and comradeship stirred his heart. "Peter," he said, "this is a lovely surprise, when did you get home?"

Paul still regarded as home for both of them, the house where they had grown up on North Circular Road, not far from the cattle market.

"You look so well Peter, you're not looking a day older than me," he said, as he regarded his brother thoughtfully. "You know, I often envied you all your sea faring travels on the Cunard Line. Sometime I still regret not grasping the opportunity of signing up like you did that day so long ago, when they were recruiting young fellows like us. But then I had met Agnes and as you know we were planning to get married. I often wondered what my life would have been like if I had gone to sea. I never regretted getting married though, I've been very happy with Agnes and we have four wonderful children, all married now with children of their own."

In his excitement Paul did not notice that his brother didn't reply. Anyway he was so elated on meeting his twin that he didn't give Peter an opportunity to get a word in. He reminisced about them growing up and playing football on the street. There was no traffic then, just the cattle being marched along by the drovers into the mart for sale.

"Do you remember us saving up for two bicycles, from the money we earned from the drovers, as we fed the cattle hay before the sales started? I didn't mind at all that the bicycles weren't new. We got a good deal from 'Spokes'. Ten shillings each and a new lamp thrown in as well," remarked Paul, "God, them were the days. Remember all the trips we took on the bikes, every Sunday a spin to Glendalough. I loved the corned beef sandwiches that Mam would make for us and oh, the Bolands batch bread covered in country butter would make your hair curl. I see you are like me now Peter, not a curl on your head, and you have a polished crown like me," he added.

"It's great though, no more trips to the barbers, or searching for that comb in the morning. In our house the comb was always missing. It was like a judicial enquiry trying to find out which of the girls had taken it to comb their doll's hair. Imagine, both of us lost our hair in the same places. You even have the same curl left over each ear as I have. I suppose that means we are still identical twins," added Paul.

All the reminiscing and familiarity gave Paul a renewed sense of importance. His granddaughter was making her first Holy Communion next week and his daughter, Trudy, had insisted that he come to the "Style for Men" shop this morning, and at least try on some suits for the special occasion. He didn't need a suit, but Trudy insisted. The suit he had, he thought, was fine and he liked it and felt comfortable in it.

Now he would get Peter to give his opinion when he tried on the new suit. Peter had always backed him up when they were young. Before he could tip Peter off, Trudy arrived with two suits across her arm.

He took and instant dislike to the colour of the first one as he saw her approach. "Trudy," he chortled, "You'll never guess who's here, look it's your uncle Peter, back home from his adventures, you remember me telling you about him, my identical twin, can you see the resemblance?

Trudy was anticipating the tussle of the century to take place as she tried to persuade her Dad to try on the new outfit. As she looked in the shop mirror at the animated image of her father all her frustration at him melted and she gently steered him away saying, "Yes Dad, we will invite Peter to lunch after you fit on your new clothes."

She knew that once she got her Dad away from the mirror all thoughts of Peter would vanish, until maybe something familiar like an old photograph, triggered a memory, and he thought of Peter again. Trudy didn't feel sad, as her Dad had a lovely time speaking to his twin brother even though it was his own image in the mirror he was looking at. Why should she disillusion him?

One day at the office

Laura had driven carefully through Abbeyleix, looking for the turn off to the small village, where the funeral was taking place. She was lost and she didn't want to be late, after all, she was representing the family.

That's what Tom had said. "You'll have to attend John's mother's funeral, he's such a good friend and we can't let him down, so you'll have to represent the family. I can't go; I'm really busy at the moment."

Laura resented going on her own, she didn't really know John that well. What really annoyed her was that Tom seemed to think she had nothing better to do. Since she lost her job last November, he had been relegating more and more things for her to do. She hardly had time to look for work now.

She had followed all the instructions he had given her that morning, but she couldn't find any sign indicating a turn off. She didn't want to ring Tom because he was going to think she was useless, but the embarrassment of being late at the funeral would be worse.

According to Tom she'd gone past the turn; she went back and found the way. Within minute she arrived at a beautiful picturesque village. Large sycamores in full bloom grew the length of the main street and continued into a small square, with a green area and seating. At one side of the square was a wooden bridge over a small stream that gave access to the grounds of the church. She found a parking space without too much trouble.

Before she left the car she checked her appearance in the mirror, a touch of lipstick was needed she decided, as she ran her fingers through her auburn curls. Nothing too bright, after all it was a funeral and she didn't want to be disrespectful, that's why she choose to wear a black two piece suit. Tom didn't like it when she wore all black, but her mother always made her wear it at her hometown funerals and she felt it was the right thing to do.

Not a minute to spare, she realised as she checked her watch. She locked her car and walked hurriedly over the bridge. As she walked down the gravel drive towards the church entrance, she studied the group of mourners but couldn't see anyone she knew.

"Excuse me; is this the funeral of Mrs Claire Murphy?" She asked a man in black suit, who looked like a mourner.

"Yes its here, are you family?" He asked with a smile, as he looked into her eyes.

"No, just a friend," she didn't know why but the man made her feel very uncomfortable. Instinctively she moved away from him.

"It is a beautiful day isn't it; with a bit of luck we will escape the rain."

"Yes, hopefully," she replied politely. What an inappropriate conversation, who is this creep? Maybe its one of John's brothers, Laura thought. Quickly she turned towards the church door but to her dismay he fell into step beside her. They walked to the church entrance in silence, then somebody called the man; Laura felt relieved and hurried into the church. She sat between two elderly ladies in a row full of people, near the front.

Soon after that the Mass started, Laura was very surprised to see the man again, but this time standing behind the priest.

The undertaker stared at Laura all the time during the Mass, he was undressing her with his eyes, and she felt his stare all over her.

To Laura's surprise, the Mass finished very quickly. It was quite obvious from the impersonal ceremony, and the priest's elegy, that Johns' mother did not attend church services on a regular basis.

As it was a beautiful warm and sunny day, all the mourners walked to the cemetery behind the hearse. Laura decided to walk beside John's wife, Susan, to be on the safe side, away from the undertaker.

After the prayers were finished, the undertaker started preparing the coffin for burial; he took the wreaths and flowers and gave them to the mourners to hold. Then while the coffin was being lowered into the ground, he took one of the bouquets and gave it to Laura. She took it in complete shock because the undertaker had to walk toward her, to give her the flowers. Laura thought that he was very obvious and she felt very embarrassed by the whole situation.

Once the grave was covered over, he took the flowers from everybody except Laura, who was holding the arrangement like a dirty nappy. He finished laying the flowers and wreaths on top of the green baize cloth, and then he went to Laura who handed him the bouquet. At that moment he caressed her hands with his, Laura could feel the touch of his warm hands on hers, he looked at her and smiled, it was only for few seconds but to Laura it felt like an eternity.

After the service Laura made her excuses to leave, she had to get away; she didn't want to be near that man. As she drove home, she still had the sensation of his hands on hers.

That evening, over dinner she told Tom about the incident with the undertaker. She was very surprised at his reaction; he had a big goofy smile on his face.

"Why are you smiling," she asked perplexed, "that man really upset me."

He reached across the table and took her hand in his and told her; "I'm glad I still have a hot wife."

Grandmother

After much waiting, electricity finally came to our farm. I had never seen my father so excited. He kept telling us how wonderful it was and how it was going to change our lives. My grandmother however didn't want it. She told my father that anything you can't see is not to be trusted. He tried in vain to have the new electric cooker installed.

No, she would have none of it. She was convinced that electricity was a fad and told him so. "It won't last, then I'll have that thing out, and it's not suitable for storing jam," jam making being the passion of her life.

"Mother," he said, trying to explain, "You'll be able to make jam day and night on this."

She looked at him in disbelief, "do you expect me to believe you can cook on that?"

"Well what about the electric light, you like that don't you?"

"Indeed I do not. You know I have to keep a sheet of brown paper around it, otherwise it will put the fire out."

I remember my father throwing his eyes up to heaven in exasperation. By the way Mother," he entreated, "let the girls listen to the radio. It's sitting over there, covered by a cloth, and only turned on for the news."

I'm afraid we were at nothing trying to tell her that it couldn't be wasted. My grandmother never came to terms with electricity. Years later, when my father got milking machines, he heard her apologising to the cows.

Her other passion was bee-keeping. She kept six hives in the orchard. There was a great variety of fruit trees, eating and cooking apples and also some crab-apple trees. The crabs made beautiful jelly. At one end she had black and red currant bushes with a few gooseberry and raspberry in another corner. A large strawberry patch produced the most delicious strawberries you ever tasted. Mind you, it was hard work keeping the slugs away from them. She wouldn't use the shop products to get rid of them. Ashes and straw were used in abundance. This certainly kept them away.

One day my father told her that beer put into containers and left between the plants did the trick. The slugs, he explained, were attracted to the smell and got into the pots and drowned. Grandmother did not like this idea and they rowed about it for some time. However, eventually she said she would give it a try, my father convincing her that dying like that couldn't be too bad. He told her that they wouldn't know, and being drunk, wouldn't care. She tried this method but gave it up after a couple of weeks, complaining to my father that she didn't really want to kill the slugs, which were after all, God's creatures. She only wanted to keep them away from the fruit. So the battle went on, the only winners being the slugs.

The bee-hives, which always looked to me like miniature houses, were situated in the sunniest parts of the orchard. She loved the bees. They were like her children. She certainly gave them more time that she gave to her grandchildren. Going to the orchard each evening, she told them of the events of the day. It there was a birth or death in the family, the bees would be told first. If this didn't happen, then according to her, there would be no honey that year and all sorts of bad luck would plague us. Definitely a disaster of some kind was imminent!

We, as children, made a laugh of this. We would sit on the garden gate and shout, "Hey bees! Have you heard the latest? The cat had kittens and Alan farted at the breakfast table!" For some reason we thought this was hilarious. We would shriek with laughter.

My father hated the bees and they in turn hated him.   When grandmother would ask, "have you told the bees, James?" He would utter an oath under his breath, knowing full well that if he did feel so inclined the bees would have none of it.   He only had to put his hand on the orchard gate and they swarmed. He'd had many a sting; that was proof enough for him.

My grandmother, on the other hand, would let them collect on her arms and they didn't bother her. She told us that our father's problem was that he didn't approach them with enough respect, so what else could he expect, and that, to her, was that. We heard so much about having respect for God's creatures, that to this day, if I saw a worm somewhere it shouldn't be, I'd pick it up and put it back in the clay.

I can think of her more kindly now. She worked really hard, out early every morning feeding fowl, collecting eggs, milking and cooking pig feed, as it was done then. The feed then had to be brought to the pig-sty, and also a good lashing of beer slops. This had been collected from a publican in town the evening before.

No sleek, model-like pigs then. You fattened them up – the fatter the better. There were generations of alcoholic pigs reared on our farm. They loved it. Mind you, my grandmother cast a cold eye on alcohol. There was a bottle of sherry kept in the house for visitors. To be offered any depended on your status in the community. The priests and ministers always got some and were forgiven for drinking it. The rest were considered raving alcoholics, and God knows my grandmother measured out her sherry very carefully. She told my father she wasn't going to be held responsible for turning anyone to drink. His reply was always the same. "I think you need have no fear on that score, Mother!"

The fairies were another thing with her. She was convinced that not only were they around the place, but that they called to see her. She told us that the best times to see them was on a warm summers evening. Sometimes the light had to be right, other times they were quite visible. She had great conversations with them, always in Irish. When we told her that there was no such thing she would give us one of her wicked looks and ask us if we knew our history. "You have heard of Tuatha De Danann, the people who went underground, now who do you think the fairies are?

We had no answer to that, fairies and history didn't interest us.

She kept her house tidy and clean but preferred to spend her time walking the fields collecting leaves, berries and twigs. We were instructed on their medicinal values, which she catalogued faithfully, along with others her mother had given her. She promised me I'd get her book of herbal cures when she died, and I did. However, some cunning relative stole it. I would love to have it now.

The local vet didn't make much money calling to our farm. My grandmother treated the cattle with all sorts of washes and potions and I have to say that we had the healthiest cattle around. My father was really proud of this. When neighbour's stock got sick he'd say with pride in his voice, "my mother will fix you up there."

No money would change hands but there would be a pint waiting in Nelson's pub in Athy, for him that night, a fact that my grandmother was ignorant of. No payment of any kind was given to her or any member of her family. She had a gift, a God- given gift, which had to be shared. My father would nod and agree with her, and in his casual way, he would hitch up his trousers as he made his way to the car, already licking his lips at the thought of what was waiting for him.

My father loved the weekly market in Athy. Farmers from around the place came to it even if they had nothing to sell. It was a great meeting place for them. During the day some of the men would go to the pub. The women usually stayed with their produce, but if the men were available, they would have a look around the shops. Market day was a chore for my grandmother, she liked the market, but hated going to town. We didn't like it because we had to get up really early, around six a.m., as all the daily jobs had to be done before we left. This was not a morning for questions!

She would dress in her 'market clothes' as she called them. A neat black coat, black hat and a blue scarf were worn, depending on the weather. The eggs which had been collected were inspected again and the special orders of brown eggs were put into boxes, each egg wrapped in news paper. She would grumble a little about this. We couldn't hear what she was saying, but it ended the same every time. She would tell us that eggs were eggs whatever the colour. She couldn't understand why town's people or, "those town's people" as she called them, thought that one egg was better than another.

Her butter was in huge demand. She was told it had a lovely country flavour! She could have sold twice the amount any market day. People would queue for it and were happy to wait the extra five minutes. Some said it had a very special flavour and wondered if it had a special ingredient in it.

I could have told them that there wasn't. Nothing only aching arms, all of us had to take out turn at the churn. Even the poor unsuspecting visitor had to give the handle a few turns. It was considered bad luck not to. Homemade jam and honeycombs were put into a tea-chest to keep them from breaking during the journey.

My father would pack apples and vegetables into sacks, the largest ones always on top. One of us had the job of making a flask of tea and some meat and tomato sandwiches. These had to be wrapped individually. "Nothing as bad as a soggy sandwich," she'd tell us.

Grandmother wouldn't dream of going to a hotel or tea-shop as they were called then. "One never knew about their level of hygiene," she would say in a very prim and proper voice. We thought that this was a huge laugh and would mimic her behind her back. When we played „tea-shop' at home my sister would say, "Now missus, before I drink this tea I would like to know your level of hygiene." We thought that if grandmother ever did visit one this would be the first thing she would ask.

Going to town didn't interest her and I'm sure if it wasn't for the market she wouldn't even know what the town looked like. She certainly didn't enjoy her trip there and let us know that when the days' selling was done she was glad to be on her way home. The countryside was the love of her life. She'd say to us, "now who would want more," never realising that we couldn't wait to leave.

Oh, to live and work in that town, sheer bliss! She hadn't much time for 'those town's people', claiming that, "we have nothing in common, they have nothing to talk about!" Meaning of course that it didn't interest her very much, that was my grandmother. I don't ever remember her throwing her head back and having a good laugh. I can't even say she saved up laughter for Christmas. It was scarce on the ground even then. Though she did smile a little when visitors complimented her on her plum pudding and Christmas cake, this seemed to please her a lot. Looking back, I think that she was lonely and needed love herself. I wonder how she would have reacted if one of us hugged and kissed her?

Harvest time and threshing days were great. There was such hustle and bustle. An air of excitement seemed to invade every part of the house. My grandmother had a spring in her step that she didn't have on other days in the year. I don't know where she got her energy. The day before, she would have cooked a full ham, apple tarts and soda bread. Beer and minerals were put into the dairy to keep them cool. When the great day dawned, water was drawn from the well to quench the men's thirst. The beer being kept until the work was done, except for a glass of Guinness with the dinner. It was a day of filling pots with water to be put on the fire for tea, and to us children it seemed as if the dinner went on all day.

My grandmother had a reputation for putting up a good meal. "Your granny knows how to fill a plate," the men would tell us. When the threshing machine eventually roared into action and the men were in position to start working, we would whoop with joy.

I have to say we were a little disappointed when the man on top of the thresher, putting in the sheaves, didn't lose and arm or a leg. We were warned every year about how dangerous it was. Under no circumstances were we let anywhere near it. We were told we might lose a limb.

It didn't escape our notice that grandmother was well respected by everyone. Even the men who worked on the farm were more inclined to listen to her than to my father. He could be a little lazy, or to put it a much nicer way, not quite as energetic as she. He had a word and a smile for everyone. I don't really know how he turned out to be that laid-back, lovely person he was. She obviously had very good qualities that we as children did not see and thankfully she passed them onto her son.

She was a woman who didn't show her feelings. Children were way down her list. 'Seen and not heard', we were told on a regular basis. She did look after our physical needs, our emotional needs, however, were not considered. But I expect that we were no different than most families of that time. Life was hard and people just got on with it.

Our mother died when we were young so our grandmother was a big influence in our lives. She was an intelligent, educated woman, whose little eccentricities made her seem odd. But, just taste her soda bread, hot from the oven with homemade butter and jam and you could forgive her anything!

Flu Blues

I dragged myself back from the edge of sleep as a loud voice shocked me into consciousness. My bleary red rimmed eyes focussed on 'my beloved', who hovered over me holding a steaming bowl of porridge.

"Here's your breakfast, eat it all up."

"But I have the flu," I croaked, "I can't eat."

"Nonsense, of course you can," he reiterated. "Didn't I eat all my meals when I had the flu?"

My legs remembered that well, all the journeys up and down stairs with the usual meals, plus hot drinks, etc.

"Mine is a different type of flu," I ventured weakly; "it needs to be starved."

"Don't be silly, sit up there now."

The porridge was shoved under my nose and a spoon into my hand. "Its lovely porridge," he said proudly, "I took special care with it, just look at the texture."

I did and nearly parted with the contents of my stomach. When I was young I had decided that porridge and I didn't agree. The porridge had the upper hand now; the only way I could snuggle back into bed was eat some. I managed two spoonfuls and that was that.

"It's lovely dear, I just can't manage anymore."

He went away muttering darkly under his breath, I'm sure I heard 'women', mentioned. I listened as his footsteps went downstairs – bliss - back under the covers, now for a nice snooze. I drifted gently for a second – the voice pierced through again.

"I forgot to ask you what you would like for dinner."

"But it's only nine o'clock."

"Well I like to be prepared early!"

"Will you just think what you might like to eat yourself?" I spoke with difficulty; my lips were dry and my throat sore. "I don't want food."

"Enough of that now," he spoke to me as if I was a difficult child, "do you want to go into decline?"

A voice inside me was clamouring to scream "would you ever get lost," he wouldn't be moved, he was determined food would cure me.

"There's some fish in the freezer or I can go down town to get you whatever you like."

Why couldn't I be treated like this when I'm well, I thought, there's a perverse spirit at work here, I'm sure. My beloved's voice brought me back from my reverie.

"I'll tell you what, let dinner be a surprise!"

Good, I thought as I pulled the duvet over my head, he was on his way down stairs again, oh no he's turning, and he's back hovering over me again.

"If you could tell me your preference for tea I can do all the shopping together."

Bleary eyed I peered at him from over the top of the duvet, and then struggled to sit up. At this stage I could feel weakness overcoming me.

"Are you alright?" He asked concernedly, "you're looking a bit green in the face. Ah, I know what you need – fresh air," he said triumphantly, throwing open the window to let a gale force wind blow through. Before I realised what he was about the bedclothes were torn off me, leaving me shaking like a leaf.

"You were perspiring all night, where are the clean sheets?"

"In the hot press," I replied shakily.

The doors of the hot press were flung open. "I can't see any sheets."

"Look under your nose!"

"I still can't see them," he yelled.

"They are in front of you, they're pale blue," I added giving him some information to work on.

"Why didn't you say that in the first place? How's a fella to know that they're not the same as the other ones. That's the thing about women, they make life very complicated. A man would have his sheets all the one colour, then no one would have to bother finding them."

The big problem then was for me to make him put the sheets on the right way up. He couldn't see any reason for the top being at the top. He decided the top could be at the side just as easily. I had a major battle on my hands but even in my weakened state I won. I didn't have the valance at my face, which he was convinced would look very well.

"I'm off to town now; will you be alright on your own?"

I had to refrain from clapping. The sound of the front door closing was like music to my ears. Then the phone rang beside me. It was a cousin of mine who hadn't been in touch with me for months.

"Is there something wrong with you," she asked, "you sound as if you have a sore throat."

"And watery eyes, runny nose, headache," I interrupted, and I wanted to add, "a husband who's trying to kill me with kindness!" I refrained.

"Oh, you poor dear," Mary replied, "you will need your rest, I won't keep you." Three quarters of an hour later she was still nattering away, when I heard the key in the lock. Mary chooses that minute to say goodbye and tell me to mind myself.

The voice shouted up, "I'll be there in a minute." True to his word he arrived with a tray bearing a mug of coffee and a cream bun. What could I say except thanks?

"I got you some lemonade – I'll bring it up in a few minutes when I've heated it."

"Oh no thanks," I protested, this is as much as I can manage."

"Look, hot lemonade never did anyone any harm; it will sweat the flu out of you."

Thought were swirling around in my mind. I was at the end of my tether, I couldn't put up with this for one more minute. With whatever strength I had left, I flung the mug of coffee in his direction, and in a hoarse, shaking voice told him to get lost. As I sunk back down under the duvet, I thought I'd better get rid of this flu quickly or I could have a broken marriage on my hands

I'm telling you this because anyone listening to his side of the story – if they were to see his bruises – would say I was a most ungrateful wretch. All I wanted was to rest and fast, was that too much to ask?

Leave Taking

[**Frank is currently working on a novel featuring** *a young man from Laois who migrates to America at the end of the Nineteenth Century. This is the opening section.*]

As Paul entered the laneway leading to the family home he savoured the sweet smell of hay. So different, he thought, from the stench of rotting fruit and vegetables that he had grown used to in Dublin's Smithfield market. He paused to take in the scene. The thatched cottage nestled among trees from which rooks swooped down to forage in the meadow. Beyond was the sweep of the Slieve Bloom Mountains. He was assailed by so many childhood memories; collecting nuts and blackberries from the hedges that surrounded the farm, bringing the cow's home for milking, catching small fish in the sweet water of the stream that flowed under the skirts of the willows that were anchored perilously to its banks, just a few yards from the house. And he remembered times when the stream turned into a torrent and overflowed its banks by the hay meadow. Fortunately those of his ancestors who had built the farmhouse had chosen a site high enough that it was never threatened by such an event.

It was many years since he had last seen and smelled this place and he may never do so again. He had left his birth place for the first time many years previously when the family became too big for the small cottage.

"You'll be better off with Aunt Breda in Dublin," his mother had said. "There's no future in farming and your aunt will see you get schooling in the city."

Paul was to discover that "schooling in the city" bore no relationship to the mornings he had spent in the small schoolroom next to the church in the village. The Brothers at the city school, who sought to inculcate the three "R"s plus scripture and Latin into the boys entrusted to their care, had little patience with the slow learning "culchie". After two years of struggling to master his lessons and receiving almost daily beatings, Paul had left.

It was not difficult to get a job as a porter in Smithfield market and he had quickly become used to the hard work involved. He had also learned a number of much more useful lessons than were on the Brothers' curriculum. He learned quickly it was possible to take home as much unsold produce as he could carry at the end of each shift – and that he could carry more than enough to feed his aunt and his cousins. He was soon able to make more money from selling fruit and vegetables to his aunt's neighbours than he made carrying sacks and crates from the warehouse to the mongers' carts.

He quickly learned, too, that some of the people he helped would show their gratitude in other ways. And that it was not worth bothering with the others. There was old Paddy Kelly who knew more about real history than the Brothers would dare to impart to their charges. Paddy told him about the great famine thirty years before Paul was born and how the population of Ireland had halved in just a few years.

Millions had starved to death and many more had scraped whatever savings they could, to travel to the Americas where, so Paddy assured him, "a man can make his fortune." Paul wondered why his grand parents, who must have lived through this horror, never spoke of it. Perhaps they thought Paul was too young – he was only ten when he left County Laois to live with his aunt in Dublin.

But Paddy said that Laois and the Midlands had not fared so badly as other parts of the country. The potato blight had devastated much of the West of Ireland because potatoes were the only crop there. Paddy's parents had been among the fortunate few who had succeeded in making the journey across country to Dublin. His own sister had been born on the journey, born dead because his mother was so weak with the hunger and the walking. Laois, Paddy said, had cattle, sheep and grain. One of the reasons people from the West went hungry was the way the English owners of the best farming land ensured that most of the produce was shipped to their homeland. But at least the Laois farmers were able to keep enough to prevent starvation. Some even helped the hungry travellers as they passed through the Midlands.

It was Paddy's insistence that America was where a young man could make a fortune which made Paul determined to make his way there as soon as he had saved enough. Now he was ready to do that. The Atlantic liners picked up passengers at Cobh and the train from Dublin had a stop at Maryborough. For Paul this provided the opportunity to make a final visit to his birthplace. But he had been surprised at the length of the walk from Maryborough station to the farm. He was glad he'd left his things in the care of the station master. Not that there was much. A cardboard case held a change of clothes, shaving gear and, hidden between the pages of a book, a thin roll of money – his savings from the years of working as a porter in Smithfield market.

As he came closer to the farmhouse he could see a man he took to be his father. The man had his back to the lane and was stooped gathering the hay into piles.

"Looks like you could use an extra hand saving the hay," Paul said.

At the sound of Paul's voice the older man started in surprise. Straightening up he set aside his pitchfork. Placing his hands on his hips he twisted his body to ease the pain in his back. Paul watched the expression on his father's face change from pain to pleasure as he recognised the son he had not seen for many years; "My, if it isn't Paul Horan come to visit his old Mammy and Pappy!"

"So it is. But it's a short stay. Youse'll not see me again till I've made my fortune!"

"With Horan luck that'll be never!"

Stepping forward to shake his son's hand the older man raised his voice: "Mammy! Come and see who's blown in from the big city! Only your oldest son! Get that kettle on and make us tea."

Hannah Horan appeared in the cottage door wiping flour from her hands on her apron. Paul, who had tried not to show his shock at the extent to which his father had aged in the years since he'd last visited the farmstead now found himself confronted by the sight of his mother. Old beyond her years, skeletally thin, white hair hanging limp around a haggard face. Still trying not to show his shock at the sight, he hoped that the brightness in his voice did not sound as false as he knew it to be:

"Ma! Is that you? And is that some of your famous soda bread you're baking?"

"Paul, son. My but „tis good to see you. And such a strapping fellow. Breda said in her letters you've been working in a market humping sacks and crates. Sure and hasn't that given you the muscles!"

Soon he was surrounded by his younger brothers and sisters, crowding into the small kitchen where Paul savoured the smell of baking bread and sipped a mug of hot strong tea.

"One at a time!" He pleaded as six people clamoured to hear about his life in Dublin.

"Give your brother some space," counselled his mother.

Eventually they all quietened down and Paul was able to answer their many questions and to tell them that he was going to America where he hoped to make his fortune.

"I'll be back some day to build a bigger house for youse all. And maybe buy some more land, too, so you can live like a lady," he told his mother later.

"And I'll be ducking to avoid the flying pigs."

Paul was pleased to hear her response for he had no serious intention of returning. He was glad that she sensed this.

"We'll never be rich so long as the English own us," she added. "I don't hold out much hope that Gladstone fellow will give us our own land back though he says he will."

"The Ulster folk'll not let him without a lot of bloodshed," his father chimed in. "Look what happened back in '85. Most of Gladstone's own party opposed Parnell's bill. Then just a couple of years ago it happened again only this time it was the Lords that killed it. You are doing the best thing young Paul. Only wish I'd done the same twenty years or more ago!"

"Danny Horan you never would have," laughed Hannah. "You would not have married me if you had."

"Reason enough in my book," joked her husband.

The Visit

Jack O'Conner was lost in thought as he stood beside the open, uninviting grave of his aunt Lizzie. Was Aunt Lizzie taking with her a secret or a gift, he pondered. He would never know now, but she had certainly influenced a major decision in his life many years before.

As the funeral prayers droned in the background, Jack thought back to his dilemma. He had been a well grounded hard working young man who had inherited a potentially good farm in Co. Kerry. Within a year he had fallen in love and married Kitty O'Shea and together they had made a comfortable home in the modest old farm house. Two sons on pushed Jack and Kitty to work all hours God sent, but the going got increasingly tough.

"Kitty," announced Jack one evening, "we have to talk."

The concern in his voice alerted Kitty.

"We can't keep going like this, all work and no return. We need help. I've given it a lot of thought and a bank loan for machinery is the only way forward. What do you think, Kitty?"

Kitty looked at her husband's face. Lines of worry were etched deep into his once smooth brow, and she was concerned for him and his well being.

"Jack, you know I hate to see you having to work so hard, and how I hate debt, but I'll trust your decision."

They sealed their agreement with a reassuring hug. When spring arrived the source of Jack's plans stood in the farm yard for all to see, a shiny new tractor which was the envy of all his farming neighbours. The first few weeks Jack was delighted, all was going well, but as the busy spring work load set in, so did an uneasy feeling. The tractor was causing him concern; there was a lot of slow starting and spluttering, and stopping mid performance. Finally one morning it failed to start at all.

Unknown to Kitty, Jack had been in town with the supplier, with no joy. "Running in problems", was their answer. At his wits end he needed to talk to someone. He didn't want to worry Kitty and pride did not allow it to be a fellow farmer. His cousin, Bill, ran a small garage in town and Jack had grown quite close to him over the years. He was always a good source of advice and most importantly a good listener.

Passing the open kitchen door Jack called out, "Kitty, I'm going to the Co-op won't be long."

As he parked on the fore court, Bill was busy replacing the wipers on a black Mercedes. The owner, a middle aged gent dressed in country tweeds and puffing on a pipe stood in the shelter of the work shop.

"Hello Jack," called Bill, "what brings you to town this time of day?"

"Desperation," replied Jack. "Should be one of the busiest days of the year, new tractor my ass! I'm sorry I didn't hold on to the horses. The damn thing wouldn't start at all this morning and I'm getting no response at all from the suppliers. Auld Dobson below in the bank is on my back and he with the deeds to half the farm. You'd think he was going to lose out!"

As Bill completed the repairs the car owner stepped forward. "Excuse me I couldn't help overhearing, may I offer you some advice?"

"Fire away," said Jack, thinking this gent does not look as if he's used to mechanics, or the workings of a farm yard. However, Jack's curiosity was aroused.

"I'm Brendan Mulcahy," he said offering Jack his hand, "and my daughter has just set up a solicitor's office in Tralee and would be glad to take up your case. If you have purchased a machine and it's not functioning as intended, there is a case to be answered." He handed Jack a small business card.

Jack thanked him and promised to give it some thought. On the slow drive home Jack could never account for Aunt Lizzie being so much in his thoughts.

She was his late mother's sister, and lived in the next village, and Jack did not see her very often. However her reputation for being sharp with the cards was well known and it was not against Father Liam's religion to engage her as fortune teller at the annual fete.

God, thought Jack, I must be desperate, yet he could not dismiss the urge to visit Aunt Lizzie.

After dinner that evening, he made an excuse to Kitty that he had to see Bill about a set of pistons for the tractor. He didn't know why but he felt reluctant to tell Kitty where he was going, he'd tell her sometime, he supposed, as he set out for Lizzie's house, where she lived alone in what was once the family home.

After two sharp knocks on the brass knocker a cheery voice called, "coming." Then Lizzie appeared. She had a pleasantly plump figure crowned with a head of red hair. "Hello Jack," she said giving him a long look. "It's been a long time and I feel it's not a social call, so into the parlour with you, where we won't be disturbed."

The room was small and had an intimate feel to it. Lizzie settled herself opposite Jack, a small table between them. She eyed him keenly. "You have a bit of trouble and worry and there are decisions to be made."

"Afraid so," answered Jack.

"Well, we will see what the cards have to say."

Jack nodded in agreement.

As Lizzie shuffled the cards she spoke slowly. "You are being hard done by and it's affecting you and yours. You have been offered advice. The advice is good. A tall building with steep steps beckons you. Inside the building you sit on the right. The ones who sit on the left produce a lot of paperwork and waffles on a lot. The one in the centre decides, and you win out. All will be well."

After a cup of tea and thanking Lizzie for her time Jack promised to call again in the near future.

As he drove home he made up his mind to visit Lisa Mulcahy at her solicitors office in Tralee the next morning.

Within weeks he was climbing the steps of the court house and sitting to the right of the judge where he was awarded a cash sum for loss of production and a replacement tractor that served him well for many years. The future certainly looked brighter.

The Amen chorus brought Jack back to the sombre reality of the graveyard and the open grave at which he stood. "Rest in peace, Aunt Lizzie," he murmured as he linked Kitty's arm and the two of them walked slowly away to their waiting car. As he got behind the steering wheel Jack's thoughts were with his aunt, and her gift for predicting the future. He never bothered going back to get the cards cut again as he reckoned once in a life was enough, anyway no one could match Lizzie's gift.

As he drove the car into the stream of traffic he wondered would he ever tell Kitty about his visit to Aunt Lizzie that fateful night, when their fortunes changed for the better.

A Grand Bit of Cake

Geraldine knew that she could never refuse her daughter anything, when Kate looked up at her with those doleful brown eyes. "Yes, I've fallen for it again," she thought, as she tweaked her daughter's nose.

"I'll see what I can do love, but you know mummy's not great at baking cakes, I always end up burning them, or they come out all lopsided."

"Oh, but please mummy, you've got to, or else the trip will be ruined," Kate replied.

She knew how important this school trip was. Kate was a great little violin player and the orchestra was trying to raise funds for an upcoming trip to England to perform in a concert there.

"Okay, I'll do my best love, but you've got to promise to do your homework properly for the next week with no complaints," Geraldine remarked.

Kate assured her that she would keep to her side of the bargain. Although with the best of intentions, Geraldine wasn't sure if she could rise to the baking challenge. Most of her baking projects, more often than not, ended up in the bin, but if she kept it simple this time she might just manage. When she was in secondary school, she used to arrive home from social science class with the most exotic of dishes, well, in the recipe book at least. She made a 'Coq au Vin' once and the whole house was violently ill for days. Her family had always been used as guinea pigs. God bless them.

She decided she'd go with a coffee cake and spent the next afternoon running around the supermarket like a mad woman, until she was sure she had all the right ingredients. Arriving home, she made certain to keep the eggs and butter out as they had to be at room temperature. Maybe that's where she'd been going wrong before. She gathered all the correct utensils and containers and eventually, the table looked more like she was preparing to perform surgery, than make a cake.

With the recipe book open on the table, she followed every step right down to the last detail. Brow furrowed and her mouth set in that funny way it always was when in deep concentration. She beat, mixed and sifted like never before. She was so intent on producing the perfect cake that she failed to notice the large amount of saliva that had begun to pool at the corners of her mouth. It only became apparent when, with a slight "plop, plop" it made its way from her mouth to the centre of the mixture.

Appalled, she hesitated a moment, but only a brief moment and continued on mixing. She'd got this far and had damn near made the perfect cake. Stopping now was not an option. Besides who the hell would notice a bit of spit?

About an hour later Geraldine sat looking at near perfection on a cake stand. She would add a cream ribbon as a finishing touch and this afternoon would bring it with her to the hall where the cake sale was to be held the next day.

"Mummy that looks fantastic," Kate said, as she ran towards Geraldine at the school gate.

"Thanks honey, I spent a long time on it, so it would come out just right." She replied with pride.

The next day, as Geraldine was waiting at the school gate, she noticed Kate walking towards her with the old bat, otherwise known as the school principal. What's up she wondered? Kate wouldn't have got herself into trouble; she was always so good at school.

"Geraldine," said Mrs Browne, with a smile, "I saw you coming in yesterday with a beautiful cake and I made sure I was first in the queue to buy it this morning."

"Oh, well I hope you will you enjoy it," Geraldine replied a little guiltily.

"Indeed I have enjoyed it. I must admit I had a sneaky little slice at lunch and passed a few pieces into the staff room as well. You must give me the recipe. I'm dying to know what you put in it. It's just so moist!"

As Geraldine walked to the car, she wondered what other recipes she might be able to improve with a few drops of "genuine mummy spit".

A Damn Good Piece of Acting

"Of course I'm missing you darling." Felicity cradled the phone against her shoulder and studied her long, red nails. "I wish you were home too, Bernard, with me." She looked up as the door to her office opened and Marco strolled in, dressed in cream polo top and black jeans that barely contained the muscular contours of his young body. He came and sat on the edge of her desk and looked at her with such intensity that her heart skipped a beat.

"I can't wait either, Darling," she said into the phone as Marco took her hand and kissed each finger in turn with long, lingering kisses that sent a shiver up her back.

"A month is such a long time darling."

She gasped sharply as Marco kissed her wrist and began working his way up her arm.

"No darling, there's nothing wrong, just a cramp in my foot. I'll stand up and move around, that will get rid of it."

She gasped again as Marco reached her neck and began nuzzling her ear.

"It's nothing darling, really. Look I'll ring you tomorrow. Love and kisses from me too."

With a long, shuddering sigh she replaced the phone on its cradle and closed her eyes.

"Oh Marco," she purred, "What are you doing to me?"

"Felicity, you drive me crazy," Marco whispered as he kissed the side of her face. "Let me stay with you tonight. Please, please," he begged, "I can't bear it anymore."

"I don't know." Felicity pushed him away and rose to her feet. She felt so undecided. Normally she was the one in control. Normally she made the decisions, but Marco was different. He set her pulses racing so much that she couldn't think straight. He'd had that effect on her from the moment she'd met him. She took a deep, calming breath and studied Marco's lounging figure.

He had walked into her office and her life barely a month ago, looking for work. An exchange student from Italy, with excellent English, he was studying architecture and had worked part time as a model and as an actor in TV commercials in Italy to supplement his income.

She had no trouble finding him work, the offers for TV commercials and modeling assignments were pouring in. But then she had never pushed so hard to find work for a male model before. There was something different though about Marco. He was so masterful. He made her feel like a young girl on her first date. None of the others ever made her feel like that. To her they were just playthings that could be discarded when she grew bored of them.

"Felicity, cara mia," he said softly as he moved towards her. "Why do you look so troubled?" His long sensuous fingers stroked her cheek as he drew close. "Your husband Bernard, he is away, yes?"

She nodded her head in agreement, unable to speak as he looked deep into her eyes. "We can be alone. We can make love together, you and me." Tilting her chin up, he kissed her full on the lips. "I will find a small hotel, in the country."

She groaned softly as his hand moved down her neck and caressed her shoulders.

"I will be very discreet, Felicity. No one will find us. Say yes Felicity. Say yes," he begged.

"Yes." Felicity whispered into his cream shirt as she leaned against his taut body. "Yes." Why should she deny herself the pleasure of Marco any longer? She had some doubts, she had to admit. Small niggling doubts that she pushed to the back of her mind. To hell with it, Marco was the best thing that had come her way in a long time; she decided as she circled her arms around his back and laughingly ran her fingers under his cream polo shirt.

Marco true to his word found a small hotel deep in the countryside. She felt comfortable with the adjoining rooms and the shared bathroom. Discreet and secluded she thought, nobody knew who she was and if Marco wasn't up to scratch he could sleep in the other bedroom, though she doubted that would happen.

Now after a wonderful intimate candlelit dinner, she was in the bathroom. Her hands shook as she slipped the cream silk negligee over her head. It slid softly over the contours of her body. She eyes herself critically in the bathroom mirror and applied more lipstick. Her hands were clammy and her heart beat like a trapped bird under her rib cage. She took a deep breath and tried to calm herself.

"The last time you felt this nervous was on your honeymoon," she told her reflection. "Poor Bernard, how easy it was to fool him."

He had wanted a virgin for a wife, and had got one with the help of some stage props and a damn good piece of acting.

But she wasn't acting this time. So what if he was years younger than her? Marco loved her, that's all that mattered, she told herself as she opened the bathroom door and stepped into the bedroom.

Marco stood by the window in the dimly lit room.

"You look so beautiful, Felicity," he said softly as he walked towards her and took both her hands in his, "so beautiful, my darling."

He kissed her gently on the lips then led her to the sumptuous bed that dominated the room.

"I can't wait for us to make love, but first I have a surprise, especially for you." He sat her down on the bed, "wait there my darling," he said as he opened the bathroom door.

What could it be? Felicity wondered as she plumped up the pillows and lay against the headboard. It couldn't be flowers; she would have seen them in the bathroom. Some jewellery perhaps, Marco was such a romantic.

"Your surprise is here," Marco said as he came into the bedroom and stood beside the bed.

"But where darling, where is it?" Felicity asked eagerly as she sat up.

"Right there," Marco pointed to the bathroom.

The bathroom door opened and a middle aged man stood there, his face set and grim.

"Bernard," Felicity exclaimed. "Oh my God what's going on? How did you get here?"

"Through the adjoining bathroom door," Bernard answered coldly. "Your bathroom services two bedrooms, my dear Felicity."

"But how did you know?" Felicity asked, "Marco, Marco what's happening?"

Marco shrugged his broad shoulders, "sorry love," he said in a thick Dublin accent as he grabbed his coat and moved to the door. "It was just another acting job."

The Hat

There were hats of all colours, shapes and size everywhere. Shapes to suit a long face, a narrow face, and a plump moon shaped face, an aristocratic face, or a dead pan face, they fascinated her. She loved hats; they gave her a sense of importance and independence. Which one would she choose? The colours were eclectic, black, grey, white and butter cream. Deep blue and pale blue, green, yellow, apricot, blush pink, pale pink and hectic red, all guaranteed to send the serotonin levels in her brain to exaggerated levels.

Every Saturday afternoon Hilda paid a visit to the hat shop. The hats were displayed openly on counter tops. She would try on various styles and hold the hand mirror at different angles, admiring her facial profile. Sometimes she admonished herself that her hair needed a new style, or her eyebrows needed a trim. Was she getting mumps she asked herself on one occasion? On closer scrutiny she discovered that she was developing a double chin. It never bothered her that she came under the close scrutiny, of the elderly shop assistant, who with much tut, tutting, and sighing would take the hat she discarded, brush it lightly then carefully replace it on its stand for display.

This particular visit was different to her other visits. She had just received an invitation to a garden party hosted by the town's Mayor. It was always a very glamorous affair, the ladies wearing their Sunday best, and the gents suited with their hankies peeping out of their breast pockets.

She gave rein to her imagination. A hat to raise her profile was a must, something that would give her an elegant bearing and catch the eye of an eligible bachelor. There was bound to be plenty of smart suited young men invited.

The first hat she tried was daffodil yellow. It had a wide brim, cocked at an angle; she thought it gave her a mysterious look. The next was deep black with a bunch of silken feathers adorning the back. The black lace pulled down over her face was a no no. It would be difficult to make eye contact having her eyes partially covered like that.

The blush pink hat was a dream, she thought, it had an upturned brim in the front; the back boasted a flowing scarf settling at the top of her shoulders. This would suit her halter neck style dress. A pity the colour of her dress was a mixture of bright red, purple, canary yellow and turquoise, she needed a more demure colour in a hat, to tone down the vibrant colours of the dress, and project its own image.

The shop assistant approached her. "Are you buying a hat?" She asked, with the emphasis on 'buying'.

returned he seemed to be resigned to his fate and didn't bark at all that night. "Ha-ha, problem solved," Sid said smiling at Helen, "isn't it great, I didn't think he'd take it so well."

However, now that he was tied up, Sparky had two tormentors, the family cats. Mr. Tom and Psycho, normally ran for cover when they saw him. But, sly and clever, it didn't take them long to work out how far the dog could travel, and they made him pay in spades for everything he had done to them. They paraded around the garden, tails aloft, eyes narrowed and what looked like an evil smirk on their faces. They would casually wash themselves just inches away from where the rope ended. The taunting was more than he could bear, and he had himself run ragged.

One day, Sparky almost caught the two cats, however, no problem they just ran up the tree. Sid and Helen are still trying to work out how Sparky made it halfway up the tree, ending up dangling from a branch. It looked so funny, but they were devastated, as not only could the dog have died but they realised they couldn't use the rope anymore. Another way would have to be found.

Sid, feeling sorry for the poor dog, decided to give him a little leeway. However this only lasted until Sid discovered that Sparky was missing again.

"Do you know what Helen, we'll have people knocking at our door, looking for puppy maintenance if we don't find a way of keeping him in," he turned to Helen, a big grin on his face. "You know, I have this thought in my head. I can almost see Sparky slicking his hair back before clearing the gate having only one thought in his head ... here I am girls, lover boy is back." Sid took a fit of laughing at this.

Helen gave him one of those looks women give men when they think they're being daft, but decided to say nothing.

That night when Sid came home from work he was all excited and he danced Helen around the kitchen. "Our troubles are over," he said, "a guy in work told me that an electric fence around the garden was the answer. Apparently the dog wears a special collar and every time he touches the fence he gets a shock. It's expensive, but it'll be great. I'll get it tomorrow."

Fence down and new collar on, Sid and Helen peeped out the window at Sparky, waiting for him to make his move. He did and it worked. The dog gave a yelp and moved away. The relief inside the house was huge, so much so they decided to open a bottle of wine. They toasted each other, Sparky, the fence and everything else they could think of. But it was not to last. Apparently pain didn't matter when it came to love and freedom, and to make matters worse his collar was stolen.

"That's it! I'm taking him to the vet myself." Helen said angrily.

"No, I'll bring him," Sid replied hastily.

"Well I'm going with you, because you're too soft and you'll bring him back with nothing done. I'm making the appointment."

An appointment was made for ten am on Thursday morning. Helen couldn't make out why Sid was fidgeting so much. She couldn't understand why he kept insisting on bringing Sparkly to the vet on his own. "I told you I am going too," she said to him.

They arrived at the surgery a few minutes before the appointed time hoping they wouldn't have to wait too long. At ten am on the dot the vet told them to leave the dog and everything would be fine.

At this stage Helen's blood was beginning to boil and she asked, "Can you please tell me why you wouldn't neuter him when he was here last year?"

"I'm afraid, Mrs Doyle it's because I wasn't asked to."

"Shush, shush," Sid was saying.

"What are you shushing about?" Helen enquired.

The vet looked from one to another, scratched his head and asked Sid to take the dog into another room.

"Mrs Doyle," the vet asked, "did your husband say he brought the dog down here before?"

"He did," Helen replied, "but he told me that you said the dog would be traumatised because of his age."

"Look, Mrs Doyle, leave the dog and I'll do what's necessary. The way it is with this operation – it's a man thing. Just leave the dog."

Sanctuary

I shall take you by hand,
Show you old places with new eyes,
I shall take you to an island,
Wrap you in cockle shells.

No trouble of the world
Will creep ashore to touch your feet,
I shall build a fire to warm night's breath
Sparks rise on dreams.

In the pool of my eye, you are near me
Oh lady come dream with me,
On a beach we'll watch white horses
Race ashore, to die at your feet.

You, with petticoat ladies, dance on waves
Disappear before I can kiss one,
Kiss me once, to taste salt
In the clutches of embraced lips

We shall grow old to dream,
As times ebb and flow runs before us
You are the compass that holds hands
In the black night there is joy.

I will pick wild fruit and silver fish,
Roll them in my palm,
No seed will hurt a tooth
When I am tired rest my bones in yours

Night Tale

On the bank I rehash a wind, to blow the same tree down,
The new morn a new breath, to die on ebbing tide.
From the shore I recall its dream, for it is only I can paint it new.
Returning, to leap upon a rock, the sprat must leave,
Swollen with the smell of silt in its gills.

I go with Brian across fields of rush,
Snipe drumming our entrance in the lush,
Brown dogs in the ring will rise tonight.
We listen to the heartbeat of the evening cool,
Brian, the best dry fly man, in the Erkina pool.

Our gaze fixed upriver, patience is the wait game,
Wind in our face, the fly man's foe, soon will die
When the sun drops like molten lead.
Our feet lodge firm in deep silt of the river
We take our stance, plaster casts of the night before.

I hear the Mallard overhead in a beat of wings
A soft whistle sound, hushing turbulent waters.
Silence descends, I gather in my emotions
Darkness creeps over the moor.

In the last glimmer of light
Little dogs rise with humping mane,
Splitting the film, lapping my boots in the ring.

I hear them suck the fluttering sedge,
Giving me a lead, filling the night to dream.
Behind me, otters whistle to each other.
A line of bubbles pass me heading for the pool

Upriver I hear a whistle calling me
Brian has a little vexed dog on a lead.
In the ring of black water, churning up a foam
The little brown dog likes to hunt the rabbit,

Feel the forged steel driving home,
This rabbit has teeth, and the pup feels its barb.
Three pounds of wild muscle kicking the net.
A tale of the night returning us to cast
Let the brown dogs rise in the ring
When the water has passed.

Summer Rain

It has rained all summer long
Making puddles of our plans,
Dampening the season's buzz.

On my window, it amplifies.
Sizzling showers beat the pan,
Then gather depressions in the gully.

Outside my door are groups,
Children mucking at the edge,
With imagination that schools.

Waves of delight splash their faces,
Time drips away,
Leaving fruit of soft rain.

Icon pools never taste bitter
For nymphs rise to surface,
In a soft drop of summer rain.

Suspicion

Unaware of the full moon above her that bathed the woods in silver light, Mary walked quickly along the familiar path through the trees, her eyes blurred with tears. Her mind was in turmoil, and her body trembled uncontrollably as her breath rose in white plumes. She hunched her shoulder against the cold night and pulled the collar of her coat tight against her neck. As she dabbed at her eyes with a crumpled tissue she wondered again for the umpteenth time how could he have done this to her, just a few days before their thirtieth wedding anniversary? She and her husband Tom had been childhood sweethearts, never once having eyes for anyone else. So what had gone wrong, what had she done for this to happen?

The cause of her distress was a note she had found in the pocket of Tom's jacket as she was getting it ready to send to the cleaners. The words of the note were burned indelibly on her brain. "Tom, will meet you Thursday as arranged for lunch, love Hannah."

She had gripped the note and sank to the floor her world turned completely upside down. Hannah was her life -long friend. They had started school together, and from that moment on had been inseparable. As teenagers they had shared every detail of their romances, preferring to make up foursomes so they could be together as they dated. Hannah was a very pretty and popular girl who was always surrounded by a flock of boys. She never married, preferring instead a single, independent life. Throughout the years they had remained firm friends, with Hannah babysitting for Mary and Tom, many a time, and on other occasions accompanying them to dinner dances and family celebrations

"God!" Mary thought, "How gullible I have been."

When Tom told her on Thursday that he had to work during lunch hour she had never suspected anything, had trusted him totally as she had done all her married life. How many time before had he and Hannah met 'on the sly'? And she was never suspicious when he said he had to work late, how stupid she felt and how angry – furiously angry at being betrayed.

She flung herself down under the great oak tree that she had always sat under when she was young and in need of comfort. Somehow the huge tree by its very size gave her courage to come to terms with any situation. This night was no different, her sobbing eased and she became very quiet. Thoughts swirled around in her mind, some sad, some angry, mostly feelings of betrayal. She would face this problem and beat it. After all she was perfectly able to live a full life on her own, why should she be dependent on others?

Resolutely she got to her feet, determined that this episode would not ruin her life. She was chilled to the core of her being, and her limbs were stiff from sitting so long. Glancing at her watch in the light from the moon she realised it was hours since she had left the house. Tom would be sick with worry, or would he? Well, to hell with him! She squared her shoulders, held her head up high and marched back down the pathway through the woods; somehow she would get through all of this.

As she neared her home, she could see Tom pacing up and down outside the open front door. On seeing her he ran towards her, his face full of concern. "Mary, where on earth have you been, I've been out of my mind with worry, do you know what time it is?"

"I don't want to talk now," Mary muttered as she walked past him into the house, "I'm tired and I'm going straight to bed."

"For God's sake Mary, at least tell me where you've been all this time," he said following her indoors. "I've been so worried, afraid that you had an accident. I didn't know what to do."

"An accident, oh you'd like that, wouldn't you," Mary hissed, "That would be an answer to your prayers." With that she slammed the bedroom door behind her.

Tom was completely taken aback, what the hell was wrong with her and where had she been? When he came in from work that evening and saw the house in darkness he thought she was out visiting friends, but when there was no warm welcoming smell of a hot meal cooking, and the fact that she had left her mobile charging in the living room, alarm bells began to ring. She never went anywhere without her mobile or at least leaving a message for him, but he was so glad to see her safely home he decided to leave well enough alone. She'd tell him tomorrow when she had calmed down.

Mary, worn out from weeping, mercifully fell asleep as soon as her head hit the pillow and didn't awaken until the alarm reminded her it was time to get up. Automatically she stretched out her hand to rouse Tom but the place beside her in the bed was empty. Fully awake now all Mary's anger from the night before engulfed her. So, he couldn't stick sleeping in the same bed as her now, his guilt must have got the better of him. Well there was no way she was getting up to get this man, this traitor, his breakfast! When he was gone to work she would hatch a plan to get her own back on the pair of them.

Tom had decided the night before that the spare bedroom was the best place for him to spend the night. Sometimes Mary got into a black mood and he had learned through the years it was best to leave her alone until she came out of it, so it didn't worry him too much that morning, when his cheery 'goodbye' didn't receive any response. "Women," he thought, "You never know when you have them!"

Mary showered and took special care with her makeup and then put on her best suit. She liked what she saw in the mirror, she still looked well for a woman her age. She was attractive and her figure was good. Any man would be delighted with her company, and there were plenty of fish in the sea for her to catch. What about the silver haired gentleman in the library? He was always asking her to have a coffee with him since the time she showed him how to send an email to his daughter in America. Philip, that was his name, well Philip, I just might have that coffee with you today!

With one last glance in the mirror she picked up her bag and looked inside. Where was her mobile? Then she remembered she had left it charging in the living room yesterday afternoon before she found that note in Tom's pocket, before her world had turned upside down. Her heart lurched and she felt sick to the stomach. Tom and Hannah, well she would show them!

As she picked up her mobile from the coffee table in the sitting room she noticed a parcel protruding from behind the corner of the settee. It was covered in a pretty pink paper with a huge white and pink bow. The bastard, she thought so he's buying her gifts now and he couldn't even be bothered to hide it from me.

Tears of fury wet her eyes. She hauled the parcel onto the settee and with trembling hands tore at the paper. "Bastard, bastard," she hissed as shred by shred, the paper gave way and there in front of her was a beautiful angora jacket in her favourite colour. As she picked it up a card fell onto the settee. Slowly her hand retrieved it, and through her tears saw the words „Wedding Anniversary'. Inside Tom had written, "Happy Anniversary Darling, I know this will fit you, Hannah helped me choose it on Thursday at lunch time. Forgive the little deception."

Mary sank on the settee, tears flowing freely down her face as she hugged the angora jacket to her chest. "Oh Tom, how could I have doubted you, and Hannah, what was I thinking of?" She was horrified and aghast when she thought of what she had been prepared to do for the sake of revenge. She'd had a narrow escape; it was the luck of God that she had left her phone charging in the living room.

Poor Tom, she hadn't even bought him a present, so immersed in self pity was she. Well that could be rectified straight away. Her step was light as she opened the front door, she'd spend the day, if she had to, choosing something special for him, he deserved it. As she strolled down the street, Mary thought on the valuable lesson she had learned, never jump to conclusions!

That night in the spotlight of the moon, Mary walked the same path she had trod the night before, this time Tom's arm was firmly around her. His hearty and relieved laugh broke the silence of the forest as Mary told him of her suspicions of the previous night. Needless to say Tom reassured her of his undying love as the moon looked on.

Moonlight Revelation

Unhindered by the night clouds the full moon shone like a beacon lighting the path through the valley. To either side steep banks rose towards heather clad moors. On the right they were in shadow but to the left the moonlight glinted on a stone wall and he thought he could discern the form of one or two sheep huddled in its shelter.

He turned up the collar on his coat and thrust his hands deeper into his pockets. The shower had passed but the wind was still bitterly cold. Looking up he could not see many stars so it seemed likely that the moon would soon disappear behind a cloud. Already he could feel the first drops of rain cutting his cheeks as another shower approached.

He'd been walking for over an hour now and reckoned it would be at least another before he reached his destination. His mind tracked back to the row that had led to his hasty departure. Why had he not simply given in and allowed Mary to have her way? Would it have been such a bad thing? Not for the first time he wished he was better at controlling his temper. Who knew what he might have done had he not stormed out of the cottage?

For forty minutes he'd strode along the deserted road that led away from the holiday cottage. Then the storm had blown down from the mountain and he'd had to take shelter under one of the few trees that were scattered across the moor.

Resting here with his back to the trunk he had begun to calm down and realise how wrong he'd been to vent his anger and use such shaming words. Now he was heading back to beg forgiveness.

The holiday was supposed to have been a chance to escape from the pressure of their lives in the city. Instead all the resentment that had blighted their lives since Mary discovered his affair had boiled over and the accusations and counter accusations had flown across the small kitchen along with some of the cheap crockery.

As Mary collected together the shattered pieces of the casserole and washed the remains of the stew from the wall and the stone flags of the floor, she wondered again if there was any future for Sean and her.

Sure he'd begun the weekend all sweetness and light, had even cooked the supper. It seemed to start going wrong over the wine. She'd wanted Merlot, he favoured Cabernet. Then she'd found the meat to be tough and stringy and he'd taken that as a criticism of his cooking. "We should have got meat from our usual butcher before we left," he'd supposed.

"You could have gone there whilst I was in the hairdresser's," she'd reminded him.

"I had work to do, you know that," he blustered.

"Oh, of course, work! With *her*!"

He wondered how it was possible to inveigle so much contempt into a single syllable. He felt his face redden as he sought to explain himself: "She is my boss. I had to brief her on the O'Sullivan contract before I left."

"I thought you'd agreed to move off that team." Her remark was more of a question than a statement.

"We did. But not until the O'Sullivan deal is completed. It would be too difficult to pass that one on to someone else."

"And how much time did you spend on O'Sullivan and how much on canoodling is what I want to know."

"Canoodling – what kind of word is that? Why can you not accept that it is over between Siobhan and me?"

"Because I know what you are like. And what she's like. It's not as if this is the first time you've been unfaithful."

"For pity's sake Mary, let it drop. As for the last time I was unfaithful, you were the one I was unfaithful with – or had you forgotten that small detail?"

In the silence that followed this exchange Mary remembered the weeks of uncertainty when they had begun their relationship and he was still married. How he kept telling her he loved her and yet kept putting off telling his wife. As she was learning now, this should have warned her of his lack of courage when it came to making difficult choices. But he had made the right choice in the end, she reassured herself. If only she could be as certain that he had once again chosen her.

She remembered how she'd discovered what was going on between Sean and Siobhan. He had been working late for several days. Pricing the O'Sullivan contract he had said. And she had believed him, suspected nothing. And then, one evening on the way home from the gym she had noticed a car identical to his parked in a secluded corner of a lay-by. The road had been re-aligned at this point a number of years ago and the curving section of the old road had been turned into a parking area, separated from the new section of road by a tall hedge.

She had pulled into the side of the road a short distance from the lay-by, reversed in a farm gateway, driven slowly back along the road and turned into the lay-by, stopping well back from the red car. Near enough, though, to see the number plate on the rear of the other vehicle before she switched off her own headlights. There was no doubt now that it was Sean's car.

She sat in the car considering the possibilities. Why would Sean park here? Was he in the car or had he left it and walked away somewhere? Or been picked up by someone at this pre-arranged rendezvous? If so, by whom? Or could he be in the car with someone else?

Her curiosity overcame her caution and she decided to see for herself. She walked towards Sean's car. If he had left it, there would be no chance of him seeing her unless he returned whilst she was conducting her investigation. If he was still in it he would be aware of her car having come into the lay-by but would have no reason to believe it was anyone he knew.

As she got nearer to Sean's car she could see that the windows were steamed up. So he was still in it! Then she noticed the rocking, gentle at first then more vigorous. My God! He *is* with someone – and they're....

She gasped and her hand flew to her mouth. The bastard! The two timing ragbag of a philandering bastard! She turned and hastened back to her own car. Once safely inside she wondered what to do. She needed to find out who Sean was with. The best way seemed to be to stay put until Sean's car left and then follow it at a discreet distance. That was how she had discovered that he was screwing his boss!

Thinking about it now she struggled to fight back tears – the last thing she wanted was for Sean to see her crying. It was Sean who was first to break the silence. "Look Mary, you know I never wanted to hurt you. I've said I was sorry so many times, what more can I say?"

Mary said nothing. She feared that were she to speak she would break down.

"Why don't we have another glass of wine?" Sean picked up the bottle as he spoke and tried to pour more wine into Mary's glass. The problem was that when he had opened the bottle earlier the cork had broken – because of the inadequate cork screw provided in the holiday cottage. Half of the cork was still inside the bottle and he needed to hold it in with the handle of a spoon as he poured. The inevitable happened and he lost his grip. The bottle fell onto Mary's glass, breaking the glass and spilling wine across the table and into her plate.

"Shit," Sean muttered.

"For God's sake! Can't you do anything right?" Mary swore as she got up from the table and rushed to get a cloth from the press.

"It was the bloody cork – and that stupid corkscrew," Sean angrily explained.

"If you had only thought to bring the proper opener," Mary remonstrated. "That's your trouble, you never think about the likely consequences of your actions!"

"You know that's not fair." Sean reached out to put his arm around Mary's shoulders. "Put that cloth down and give us a kiss."

"Get away!" Mary pushed him off roughly. "Don't you dare think you can get round me like that? I've had it up to here with you and your infantile behaviour."

Sean felt his face redden. His mind was in turmoil. He couldn't think what to do. One part of him wanted to hit out and strike Mary. Instead he picked up the casserole from the centre of the table and flung it as hard as he could at the wall. Then he grabbed his coat from the hook on the back of the door which he opened and strode through, slamming it behind him.

Sean saw the headlights swinging across the sky as the car came speeding down the valley towards him. He wondered why Mary was driving away from the cottage. It was not like her to drive with such reckless speed. Was something wrong? And why was she still speeding as she rounded the bend from which she must have been able to see him? The car made no attempt to slow down and he was forced to leap into the ditch as it roared past.

He got up and turned to watch as the car disappeared from view behind an outcrop of the mountain. He had to get back to the cottage as quickly as possible. He broke into a jog. He remembered how he had been taught as a youth in the scouts to alternate five minutes of jogging with five of brisk walking in order to cover as much ground as possible as quickly as possible. In this manner it should be possible to reach the cottage in fifteen or twenty minutes.

What would he find when he got there? What had Mary done? Why had she left in such a hurry? And why had she ignored him?

Another thought was nagging at the back of his brain. Perhaps it wasn't Mary driving the car! It was his car, of that he was certain because the lane ended in the front yard of the cottage; there was no way for a vehicle from any other place to be on the road. But Sean was aware that there was a high security prison in the next valley. He had never been concerned about this since escape was supposed to be impossible and it was many years since the last time such a thing had happened.

But the way the car was being driven made him increasingly certain that it was not Mary at the wheel. In which case was it wise to keep heading back to the cottage? Should he head in the other direction to find a point where he could use his mobile phone to call for help? No, he needed to find out what had happened. Maybe even now Mary was lying in agony on the floor of the cottage and needed him.

He increased the pace of his running. He needed to get to the cottage quickly. But he needed to conserve his energy so that he could quickly come back down the valley as soon as he knew what the situation at the cottage was. Oh how he wished he had never given in to Siobhan's seduction! He didn't even like the woman. He disliked intensely her lack of business ethics.

He had argued with her over the handling of the O'Sullivan account. They were on the way back from a meeting and Sean had pulled the car into a lay-by to – as he put it – "have it out with her". The argument had become increasingly heated and then, to his consternation the passion of their dispute had given way to passion of a different kind. Afterwards both had vowed never to work together again. He would be given free rein to run the O'Sullivan account with minimal input from Siobhan. And when the account was completed Sean would transfer to Patrick's team.

He was ashamed of his weakness in allowing himself to give in to his lust. This was nothing like his feelings for Mary. Although he had been married when he had met Mary, the marriage was already effectively over. He and Sally had married too young. Whilst he knew several contemporaries who were no older when starting out in married life and whose marriages had survived, he and Sally simply couldn't make it work.

His relationship with Mary was very different. It wasn't that they had so much in common. Rather it was the attraction of opposites and stronger for that. Where life with Sally had become boring and predictable, his time with Mary was constantly throwing up surprises. Now he could not imagine life without her. And the thought that she may even now be lying injured in the cottage filled him with remorse for his stupidity and apprehension at what he might find.

After she had finished clearing up the mess and set the dishwasher going Mary decided to have a shower. She hoped that the fresh herb scent of the shower gel and the rush of water would help wash away some of the unpleasantness that the failed dinner had created. As she dried herself and wrapped a warm bathrobe around her she heard the grating noise of the kitchen door hinges. She was surprised that Sean was back so soon. On previous occasions when he had run away from a row he had stayed away for two or three hours. Now she supposed the foul weather had driven him home. She hoped that his mood had mellowed.

"Back already?" She stopped almost before she had begun her welcome speech. Facing her as she entered the kitchen was not Sean but a stranger. A beard and long dark hair, wet and matted, were the first things she noticed. Then she saw the kitchen knife pointed towards her.

"The keys!" The man uttered just two syllables. Then repeated them, louder, and added a third. "The keys! Now!"

"K..keys? What keys?"

"Car!"

Mary moved to the drawer in the sink unit. Without taking her eyes from the intruder and his weapon she groped among the odds and ends until her trembling fingers found the keys to Sean's car. Her mind was in turmoil. She struggled to control the mixture of emotions that overcame her. Anger at herself for not ensuring the door was locked and bolted; anger at Sean for leaving her alone and vulnerable; anger at herself for feeling vulnerable. Over-riding all of this was the dread she felt at what the next few moments might hold. She must get the stranger out of the cottage. If giving him the car keys was what it took, so be it. And yet, without the car how would she and Sean get back to civilisation? There was no fixed phone and mobile coverage was non-existent this far from a mast. They would have to walk for several miles before they could get a message to the outside world.

"Quickly!" The man thrust the knife towards her menacingly. She grabbed the keys and threw them towards him. They landed on the table from where he took them before running out of the door, still brandishing the knife. She heard the engine of the car burst into life followed by the sound of gravel spraying from under its wheels as it raced away from the cottage.

Mary collapsed into the leather easy chair in front of the fire and began to sob, her shoulders heaving. If only she had not spoken so harshly to Sean he would not have left her alone to face the intruder. Where was he now? She wondered. He would surely have seen the car. What would he make of it? He would hardly suppose she was driving away so furiously – she was a cautious driver.

She decided it was time to pull her self together, get dressed and, if Sean was not back by then, venture out herself to meet him. After all, they would have a long walk to find a mobile phone signal in order to summon help. Better if he did not have to come all the way back to the cottage from wherever he had got to in his rush to escape her tongue.

As Sean approached the cottage he saw the light from the window go out. Then he thought he heard the sound of the door hinges as it was opened and then shut. Clearly someone was able to move about, but was it Mary or had there been more than one escapee? He ducked behind the wall until he was sure that the approaching figure was indeed Mary.

"Thank God!" He stepped forward and then stopped as she recoiled.

"My God Sean, you scared me half to death! Thank God you are here." Now she relaxed and allowed Sean to shelter her in his strong embrace.

"Mary, my Mary, are you alright? What happened?"

"I'm sorry, he had a knife. I let him take the car."

"Never mind the car, what about you? Did he..."

"No. But he gave me a hell of fright. Thank heavens you are here now. Promise me you will never run away again, no matter what happens between us."

"Never, I promise. Mary I don't know what I would do if I lost you."

Lazy Days

That time of year again,
Off to Castlegregory,
For lazy days under canvas
And midnight feasts by gaslight.

Tent tied to roof rack,
Provisions in the boot
Six excited children
Crammed in the back

On the open road,
Tyres hum a driving song.
Looking through the window
Counting sheep and cows,

"Are we there yet," we chorus
Knowing full well, NO
Down the narrow roads
Over bumps so slow

I spy with my little eye
Something beginning with P,
As baby brother pukes,
From too much fizzy pop

Unscheduled stop at lay -by,
For T- shirt change and toilets,
Milk and bread from local shop
Last leg of the journey now

A wrong turn on a winding road,
Dad soon puts that right,
Campsite sign, seen up ahead,
Sets little hearts a-pounding

The car comes to a halt,
Our destination, journeys' end,
In reverse sardine formation
Tired bodies clamber out

Gas stove taken from the boot,
Mum puts the kettle on
While tent poles and ground sheets
Lie waiting on the grass.

Little legs start running
Towards a sandy shore,
They have no care for tent poles,
As toes dip into water.

Congratulations Jim

With a contented sigh Meg huddled closer to Jim under the protective foliage of the chestnut tree as the rain poured down from a leaden sky. She loved the feeling of privacy the green canopy provided as it sheltered them from the rain, like they were the only people in the world. It could rain for as long as it liked, she didn't mind. She could stay here forever!

"Summer weather how are you!" Jim remarked in his gruff voice as he pulled the collar of his light, summer shirt closer to his tanned neck.

Meg followed the movement of his brown hand as it fiddled with the shirt. She'd been right about the colour; lemon suited his swarthy complexion and black hair. His hand moved to his hair, pushing the wet curls back from his forehead. She watched the movement, fascinated as his bulging muscles strained against the short sleeve when he moved his arm.

There was so much strength in those arms; he could lift her right over his head if he had a mind to. Her eyes travelled to his handsome face, now set in a deep scowl, dark eyebrows drawn together over startling blue eyes.

"It'll be over soon," she comforted, "look, you can see the edge of the cloud, it's moving away."

"You have an answer for everything, haven't you," he growled, "Does anything ever annoy you?"

"It's only a drop of rain," she protested, "I got wet too." Her heart sank. The last thing she wanted tonight was Jim Touhy in bad humour.

He scowled at her. "Yeah, you look like a drowned rat. As a matter of fact you look ridiculous. What did you do with your hair?"

Tears welled in her eyes at his hurtful words, and her spirits sank even lower. Mark had styled her hair differently today so she would look her best for tonight. He said it flattered the shape of her face and as an extra bonus made her look a little taller.

She'd been delighted with the result when he held the mirror at different angles to her head so she could view the effect. "I think I'll get it styled like this in future," she said, slipping him an extra two Euros as a tip.

Jim hadn't mentioned her hair when she met him in the park as arranged, or her new dress and shoes. But then Jim wasn't great at paying compliments. The only time he ever complimented her was the first night she sneaked him in through her bedroom window after the disco.

"You've the most beautiful brown eyes I have ever seen," he whispered into her ear as he lay beside her, "a man could drown in their softness."

Granted, both of them were fairly drunk that night but she did believe him when he said he loved her. Now as she looked up at his scowling face she wondered where all the tenderness he'd shown that night had gone to. She forced herself to smile. "When we get to the pub I can fix my hair. It only got a bit wet."

It was at times like this when she wondered if her sister Bertha wasn't right after all. "He'll break your heart," she was always saying, "have nothing to do with him Meg he's a complete waster. Get away from his before it's too late."

Bertha never saw him the way she did. She never saw how much fun he could be. Or the way he could charm his way into a crowd of strangers in a bar and end up being invited to a party in someone's house by the end of the night. He was exciting, good company most of the time, though she did have doubts at times, especially when Bertha started at her. She'd tried to explain several times how she felt but Bertha wouldn't listen. Sometimes Meg wished she'd leave her alone and stop mothering her; let her lead her own life and make her own decisions. After all they weren't children anymore.

What would Bertha say if she knew how far the relationship had developed? She'd have to tell her soon, after all she was three months gone now and would soon begin to show. She didn't relish that undertaking; Bertha would go ballistic. But first she had to tell Jim Touhy and she wanted to do that tonight when he had some drink taken.

Standing before the mirror in the ladies Meg pondered her predicament, as she re-arranged her hair. Jim's mood had lifted, but then it always did when he met Des. Des had a calming influence on Jim, which was lucky for her because Jim Touhy in a bad mood she wouldn't wish on anyone. She liked Des; he was always nice to her. It's a pity she couldn't say the same about his wife.

"Anyway Meg, how are you going to tell Jim about the baby?" She asked her reflection as she checked her make-up. "Jim, guess what? I'm pregnant." No, too quick, too flippant. "Jim I've great news for you, we're going to have a baby!" No, that wasn't right either. She couldn't spring it on him like that. She could bring the conversation around to Des and Rita's new baby; Jim was very taken with the child at the christening. Or was that just because Des asked him to be the godfather?

Rita wasn't too happy about that. For once there was nothing she could do about it; Des was adamant, and for the first time since she knew them, he'd stood up to Rita. Didn't himself and Jim go back a long way, he said to her. Haven't they been mates since they were children?

"I could have told her that if she'd climbed down off her high horse, but then she's too grand to have a decent conversation with the likes of me. She doesn't like Jim either; I saw her face when she thought nobody was looking. She's all over him when Des is around, chatting and flirting to beat the band. She'd make you sick!

Of course Jim laps it up, thinks she's classy if you don't mind. All that dyed blonde hair and fake tan. He's always holding her up to me as an example. Rita this and Rita that, of course if I say anything against her I'm jealous. One of these days he'll see her for what she really is," she thought.

Meg put her make-up back into her bag and stood sideways in front of the mirror eyeing her shape as she moved her hand in a circular motion over her tummy.

Wait until she finds out about me being pregnant, Des will get it in the neck for associating with my kind. She sighed deeply. First she had to tell Jim. Later on back in her room, she promised her reflection as she walked to the door.

"You're looking very well tonight, Meg. I haven't seen that dress on you before." Des remarked as he pulled out a bar stool for her.

Meg's heart warmed with gratitude, she could always depend on Des to lift her spirits.

"Here, sit up on that and we'll get you a drink. Will you have the usual?"

"Thanks Des, a glass of lager will be fine. I'm glad you like the dress." She glanced quickly at Jim, "I got it today."

"Well it certainly suits you, you look radiant, doesn't she Jim?" He said.

Jim looked at her over the top of his pint, "yeah, she doesn't look too bad," he admitted, "she cleans up well." He grinned at Meg as Des hit him a playful thump on the back, "you wouldn't want to tell her that too often or she'll get a swelled head," he added winking at her.

Relief flooded over Meg as she watched them laugh and chat. Jim's earlier mood had gone completely. Things were looking good for their important chat later on. That only left Rita to contend with. With that in mind she turned to the tall blonde that sat opposite her smoking a cigarette, her tanned legs crossed and bared to mid thigh. "Hello Rita, how are you? It's very quiet here tonight, isn't it?"

Rita regarded her through a haze of blue smoke, a look of barely concealed disinterest on her sharp features. "I didn't think you'd be here tonight," she said, "it's not one of your usual nights, is it?"

"No, we usually go to the pictures on Wednesday night," Meg answered pleasantly, "but tonight we decided for a change we'd have a drink." Not that you're interested, she thought taking a long swig from her glass of lager.

Rita's eyes flicked briefly over Meg. "Well, what's the occasion," she demanded, "are you going to tell me or do I have to ask Jim?"

Meg's heart leaped. "What occasion? What do you mean?"

"Well you've obviously gone to the trouble of getting your hair styled differently, and the new dress." She leaned across and fingered the material. "You got it on the market didn't you?"

"So what if I did," Meg answered defensively, "what's wrong with it?"

"Nothing if you like shopping on the market." Rita smirked as if at some private joke then pulled hard on her cigarette and blew the smoke in Meg's direction. "Personally I wouldn't shop there if it were the last place on earth." With a long, red fingernail she tapped her cigarette over an already full ashtray then brought her hand close to her face and dangled the cigarette over her mouth. Her eyes narrowed as she leaned in close to Meg and spoke in a low tone. "A bit of advice Meg, men of Des and Jim's calibre like to see their women well dressed. It reflects on them as men of the world, you understand what I mean?"

"I'm sure I do!" Meg muttered through clenched teeth as she grabbed her glass of lager from the counter.

"Men of the world how are you! Des Grogan and Jim Touhy men of the world? Oh, if only this was your neck I had my hand around, she wished as she downed the contents of the glass. "Steady on Meg; don't let her rile you, that's what she wants. Slowly she put the empty glass down.

"Jim has never complained about the way I dress," she stated.

"Of course not, but then he wouldn't, would he?" She laughed sharply and glanced across at the men who were deep in conversation.

"Jim's too nice to say anything to you. But when you're dressing for a special occasion, like tonight for example," she added staring intently into Meg's face; "you should make a special effort, shouldn't you?"

Meg's face reddened under her scrutiny. She knows. She knows there's something up.

"There's no special occasion," she stuttered, "I just felt like dressing up, that's all." She eyed her empty glass wishing it were full.

Rita regarded her through half closed eyes.

"I know what it is." She wagged a triumphant finger at Meg, "you're getting engaged, aren't you? That's it," she added, "Jim kept that one close to his chest, never told his buddy."

She turned to the men, "Jim, hey Jim. You're the quiet one!"

Jim cocked his head up, looked at Rita then Meg, "what? What did you say?"

"Nothing Jim," Meg answered quickly, "nothing at all."

"Des guess what," yelled Rita.

"Will you hush up Rita, for God's sake!" Meg caught her roughly by the arm and shook her, "you don't know what you're talking about."

"What are you two up to?" Des enquired, "What are you smiling about Rita?"

Meg glared at her as she released her arm. "Don't mind her. Rita's imagination is working overtime tonight."

"What's wrong with you then?" Jim asked her, "You're fierce flushed looking."

"I think I've embarrassed her, Jim," Rita said, coyly fluttering her black eyelashes as she spoke. She leaned across the bar in front of Des and placed her hand on Jim's arm, "I thought you were getting engaged."

"For Christ's sake Rita," Des said impatiently, "would you stop trying to cause trouble and mind your own business."

"Jesus," said Jim looking at her in disbelief, "engaged? Me?"

"Yeah, imagine that Jim, aren't I terribly silly?" She sniggered.

"Stop it Rita," warned Des, as he looked at Meg's crestfallen face, "I'm telling you now, drop it!" He shoved a fresh drink in Rita's direction, "here get that into you and leave Meg alone."

"What have you been saying Meg?" Jim demanded, his eyes glinting dangerously. "Have you been going around behind my back telling people we're getting engaged?"

"No I haven't." She was appalled. How could he think that of her? How could he not trust her? She had a sudden vision of her sister Bertha saying; "I warned you Meg, I told you what he's like." She brushed the vision away. No, he was just upset with Rita. "Don't you trust me Jim? Are you going to believe someone else over me?" She stared earnestly into his face, "Rita's winding you up. Like I said already, her imagination's working overtime tonight."

"Meg is right Jim," said Des handing her a fresh drink. Rita can be a proper bitch when she's trying to cause trouble. Can't you?" He turned a disgusted look on his wife.

A malicious smile played on Rita's lips as she leaned back against the bar and lit a fresh cigarette. "Am I now?" She blew a stream of smoke over their heads, "well, I still think Meg's up to something; she's looking very uncomfortable for one that has nothing to hide."

Meg's heart pounded as the three of them fixed their gaze on her. She released her glass of lager from her sweaty hand, onto the bar and wiped her hands on her thighs. Her eyes flitted from one to another of their faces, aware of Rita's triumphant smirk, Des's curious gaze and the icy glitter in Jim's eyes.

"Well Meg," he said, "out with it. What are you hiding from me?"

Beads of sweat broke out on her forehead. This wasn't the way it was supposed to happen. She'd never forgive Rita, ever. She looked pleadingly at Jim. "Oh, Jim I didn't want it to be like this. I wanted to tell you when we were alone later on." Her stomach lurched and the sour taste of bile rose in her throat. She gagged.

"Tell me what," Jim shouted at her, his face inches from hers, "what?"

"Oh God," she said jumping down off the stool as a wave of nausea hit her, "I'm going to be sick."

"Jesus Christ," she heard Rita shriek in the background, as she rushed to the toilet, "I know what's wrong with her, she pregnant! The silly little cow is pregnant."

"What are you saying?" Jim bellowed.

"Rita, you're nothing but a bitch," said Des in disgust.

"Congratulations Jim!" Rita's laugh was spiteful as she faced Jim, "what do you think of your little Meg now? Poor Jim, she's going to make you a daddy!"

The Devil you Know

Anita loved her straw hat. She always wore it on the beach. The brim helped to keep the hot sun's rays from burning her face. All the beauty magazines advised that if you wanted to be wrinkle free you kept your face in the shade.

Today, this advice was the least of her thoughts. She wondered if the postman had arrived yet. All this waiting was getting very tiresome. Time was moving on, she had only two more days to spend in her holiday cottage, before the timeshare holiday makers arrived. She had her plans to make, and she needed them in place before she went back.

She had just had a swim in the balmy waters of the sea, which literally lapped up to her back garden. Under her wide brimmed hat, her hair dripped down in a tangled mess between her shoulder blades. The warm sun dried her brown limbs as she slowly walked along the sandy beach towards her holiday home.

She would have to start packing when she got back. All her clothes were neatly folded beside her travel bag. This morning, as she headed for the beach, she had draped herself in a white bed sheet over her bikini. Always minimalistic, she didn't need to disturb the neat pile of ironed laundry that she intended packing after her trip to the beach.

Opening the narrow hall door, her eyes fell towards the colourful floor mat. "Oh golly!" She exclaimed. "At last, some correspondence." Bending forward, to pick up the vellum envelope, her straw hat fell to the floor. Impatiently, she jammed it back on her head. Fingering the heavy vellum envelope she wondered if a photograph was enclosed. Her heart flipped with nervousness and she felt guilty again for contacting the dating agency.

Really, she was quite happy with Hector. She would never have sent her details to the dating agency, except in a fit of pique; she had decided to test the field.

If only he would pop the question and not keep her dangling on a thread. After all it was ten years now since they started going out. A girl couldn't be blamed for getting itchy feet. She stared at the envelope in her hand, should she just tear it up and forget about her options?

How long was she prepared to wait for Hector to pop the question, knowing him it might never happen? No, she had her life to consider. Slowly she lifted the flap back with her finger. "No harm done," she told herself, "it's only a letter, and he need never know."

In the meantime she would continue to drop subtle hints about all their friends settling down.

With trembling hands, she pulled at the contents of the envelope, out came a letter of introduction. Before she could read it, a passport size photograph floated onto the doormat. As she lunged forward to pick it up, her straw hat fell off again. Astonished, her gaze fell on the handsome face in the photo. All thoughts of retrieving her straw hat vanished, as Hector smiled up at her.

The Widow

I'm glad the funeral is over, I always secretly wished for his death, I thought it would make me happy; but when the time finally came I couldn't feel anything, just a deep emptiness inside me.

I'm not even sure if the children are grieving. He wasn't really a good father; he wasn't a good husband or a good person. As far as I know, they will be thinking the same about me when I die. Yes I'm not a good mother, I didn't want to be one in the first place, and probably I'm not even a good person either. I tried to be a good wife but I had to survive. In trying to succeed I became greedy.

I was the eldest daughter of an Irish man and a Spanish woman; we were living in a small community in Mexico. My father had a farm and the only shop in the village, where he used to sell all the goods produced there. He traded cattle and pigs; he got supplies, groceries, draperies and any single thing that could be exchanged for money.

My parents met in Spain during the civil war; after they got married they immigrated to Mexico during the Franco dictatorship.

My mother did not believe in educating women. I was allowed to go to school for two years. When I was able to read, write and do basic arithmetic work, I had to leave school. My parents believed that women shouldn't have any academic knowledge. They where faithful to the principle, "if a woman learns Latin she will not get a husband", under that parameter I was taught how to rule a house.

My mother had two maids one in charge of the kitchen and the other in charge of the cleaning. I learned to cook, sew and boss servants, I was quite happy with life on the farm. I always had the best of everything. When my mother wanted to go shopping we went in a private air plane to the capital where we got hats, gloves, shoes and material to make dresses in beautiful vibrant shades. We never brought materials similar to the ones sold at the village shop, so that nobody in the village would be wearing the same garments as us.

When my younger brother was ten he was sent to a boarding school in Spain, within three years the other two where sent away too, leaving only a toddler and a baby as my sole company. My mother didn't want her sons to be farmers, they had the means, so the boys had the privilege of an education I was denied.

At fifteen I was very lonely. We where always considered outsiders in the village and because I didn't go to school I couldn't get close to any of the girls. I was longing for a sister or a friend but the only person near by was

Carolina a handicapped girl, daughter of one of the servants, who used to walk around the table when we were eating, I was not allowed to befriend her.

Soon after the last of my brothers was sent abroad my father decided to change business. He sold the farm and the shop, and became a transport tycoon. He knew there was a need to connect all the villages with the city, so he bought buses and created routes going to the farthest village in the state, it was an instant hit. He made a lot of money; he owned more than fifty buses, not bad for a man who never drove a car. Back on the farm he used to go everywhere by horse.

When the family moved to the city he had a driver. I was really happy about the move, finally I was going to be able to meet people and make some friends, have a boyfriend and go to dances and parties. I was considered a beautiful girl and my parents were well aware of that. My expectations of living in a city where shattered immediately. To my dismay I wasn't allowed contact with anyone. I was forbidden to go to parties, or have any friends. I was allowed to go to the shops once a week with my mother, and every Sunday morning, I was taken by my parents to six o'clock Mass in the parish church.

This Mass was usually populated by the very old and infirm which suited my parents as they didn't wish me to be seen. Soon, rumors started that in San Miguel parish, there was a beautiful girl who was kept prisoner in her own house.

I longed to stroll through the streets and linger at shop windows, or walk to the park and sit for a while under a shady tree, even go to the church and light a candle, but I wasn't allowed that privilege. So every day I used to stand by the window, watching people pass by, delivery boys, maids running for errands, mothers with children, how I envied them their freedom. Then one day as I stood by the window, a well dressed, handsome young man passed slowly by. I was intrigued, who could this stranger be, he certainly didn't live on the street.

I thought no more of it until the next day, when I stood at the window and he passed by again. Curious now, I called one of the servants and asked her did she know who he was. His name was Francisco, his family was very wealthy and they lived on the big house on the hill. I knew the house well, for we passed it on our way to church every Sunday morning.

Francisco started passing by the house at the same time every day. He had heard the rumors about me and decided he had to see if they were true. He would lift his hat and smile at me, bending down his head a little bit. At first I was flattered and welcomed the attention, as it broke the monotony of the day. Then I found I was counting the hours until he would arrive, I was infatuated with him, and I wanted to be closer to him so badly, then, one day, I did the unthinkable. I smiled at him.

The following week my parents were visited by the bishop and a nun from the convent called Sister Christina, who acted as the bishop's secretary. The holy envoy asked my parents to allow Francisco to court me. They couldn't say no, especially when they found out that Francisco's family was very wealthy.

Within three months we were engaged, during that time we never were alone, my mother or one of my younger brothers was always there. I wanted to be just with him, but that wasn't the right thing to do at the time.

The wedding was the social event of the year. Everyone who was somebody was there, and my brothers sent me good wishes and presents from Europe. My dress was made with the finest silk and lace, beautiful pearls adorned my hair, and I was holding a magnificent bouquet of white orchids. It was like a fairy tale.

When we came back from the honeymoon we moved into a small house in another part of the city. It was then that Francisco began to show his true colors. Absence, alcohol and women; in all their forms, blonds, brunettes and red heads. Waitresses, nurses, even the next door neighbor was part of the non stop sequence of affairs. I tried to leave, but I didn't have a place to go.

I went to see my parents; they were horrified when I told them I wanted to leave him. They wouldn't listen to me, I was told that it was my fault, after all if I didn't look after my appearance, what did I expect my husband to do.

"Don't let yourself go, always be pretty for your husband," my mother preached, "Just remember, divorce is not an option. You can't come back. Once you get married you belong to your husband, not to your parents."

My father left the room without saying a word and banged the door behind him, leaving me with my mother. She came closer and almost whispering she told me, "If you want to keep your husband happy do everything he wants you to do."

I left their house and with that the only hope to be free again. I tried to make sense of their words but, I couldn't understand why life was so hard, or why I couldn't count on my own family, I felt so lonely I wanted to die.

I walked for hours under the sun. When I got home I couldn't eat. I was sick for days. Nine months later my first son was born. My mother came to see me. "I hope you left behind all those stupid thoughts of leaving your husband, because a woman alone with a kid gets nowhere."

Seven more children came, year after year. Somebody told me that I was blessed with the gift of fertility, but I knew I was dammed with it. I didn't enjoy been pregnant or holding a baby in my arms. Francisco used me as he pleased, I felt violated every time. I never got a word of love from him or any sign of affection, and I found it difficult to love my children who where the product of countless assaults on my person.

Despite my indifference and lack of care they all survived into adulthood. They had the usual childhood illnesses, measles, chicken pox, one of the boys had his appendix out and another broke his leg when he fell from a tree. They weren't good students in spite of the fact that they were intelligent, I didn't have the interest in their education that I should have had when they started school, and because of that they all had to repeat first class.

Every time the children came home with their school reports Francisco would rage at me and call me a bad wife and mother. "Had I no respect for him or his family name, did I not realize the shame I was bringing on him? What sort of woman was I not to want my children to do well?"

I wasn't capable of caring about him or the children I just felt empty inside. The children soon learned not to come near me for any of their needs, either emotional or physical. I left their welfare strictly in the hands of the servants. There were never any real problems with them, even though two of them were bed wetter's, when they were small, but they grew out of that.

During the time when the children were very small, Francisco would to give me a daily allowance to get food. He told me the reason for this was I was useless at managing money, or the house and he would leave that in the capable hands of the housekeeper. Sometimes he would go away for days, without telling me where he was going or how long he'd be away. I wouldn't have enough money to feed myself or the children, and in spite of the fact that I didn't love them like I should, I wouldn't let them starve. I couldn't plan a budget because I didn't know when he was going to get back.

At the beginning I didn't know what to do; I didn't want to ask my parents for help. I knew Francisco did it on purpose to make me feel bad about myself. Then I got the idea to start saving, I would economize, buy cheap cuts of meat, and lots of vegetables, fill the kids with lots of rice and potatoes. That way I started my little stash. During my husband 'trips' away, we were not hungry anymore. And to have money of my own gave me a sense of independence that I never felt before.

My father in law died unexpectedly. And we moved to his house to take care of my mother in law who was in a wheel chair. The house was beautiful, much bigger than I realized, with a huge garden, and plenty of space for the children. My parents were delighted; I was moving up in the world, as for me, my prison got prettier. Soon after we moved, a woman came to the house one morning, looking for my father in law; she was devastated when I told her he was dead.

At the sight of her sorrow I offered to help. She said she needed money to go out of town to her sister's funeral and then she told me; "if you lend me the money I will pay you the same interest that I used to pay to your father in law, I have this ring, I will leave with you." It was the beginning of a new career.

I took over my husband's family business and he never found out. He was busy philandering and drinking, I never showed any sign of my increasing fortune, the meals where the same and I couldn't stop saving. I became greedy; to have more money became my target in life.

I never lent money without a collateral and I became an expert in jewellery I was able to recognize good stones and the quality of gold. I got wedding, graduation, and engagements rings, necklaces, earrings, and watches, even property deeds. I didn't have any scruples; people had to pay interest every month, after six months they had to pay the principal, if they didn't pay the collateral was mine.

Making money made me happy. It was my reason to be, I hated to live in that house, the children didn't give me any satisfaction and my repulsion for Francisco arose every day. Nevertheless I became indifferent and distant; I didn't allow him to go near me.

The first time I refused him I was terrified he would beat me, but he was so drunk he just fell asleep. I was feeling more confident because I knew he couldn't do anything to hurt me. I was used to his insults and public humiliations which in a way made me look like the devoted mother I never was.

One day when I was giving him breakfast, he complained because the eggs where a little bit overcooked. I told him that if he didn't like the way I was cooking, he should make them himself. He was furious; he took the plate and fired it against the wall. The fried eggs slid down the wall leaving a yellow streak in their wake. The dog got close and began to lick the mess. That morning my nieces where there having breakfast with the children, and I could see the horror on their faces.

My parents died within a year of each other. Now that they were gone I knew it was time for me to live my life. A few days after my mother's funeral, I found a small two bedroom apartment near the centre of the city; it was beautiful; full of light with big windows and a balcony facing the main square. Every morning after the children went to school I went there to make that place my real home, in only a few weeks the place was ready. I was thirty nine, it was time to finish with twenty years of misery.

The morning of my departure Francisco had one of his usual hangovers he was sitting in the kitchen sipping a cup of strong coffee waiting for his cooked breakfast, one by one, the kids came in and started to grab cereal and milk, my mother in law was in the corner of the kitchen chewing a piece of bread, quietly contemplating the room full of noise and laughter.

I stood by the window watching them all and suddenly the room felt small, dark and dirty. I was looking at the overcrowded white table in the green kitchen and I couldn't feel remorse, I was going to leave and nothing could stop me.

I couldn't tell them; I don't know why, I felt pity for the children. I looked at them and I saw twenty years of my life gone down the drain, it was better to leave without saying goodbye. I didn't want them to see me leaving.

After breakfast everyone went about their daily activities, I went to the bedroom and took my handbag, the rest of my things were already in my apartment. I left the keys of the house on the dresser, applied some lipstick and walked out of the bedroom, thinking that it would be the last time I was going to cross that door.

Francisco was in the office, looking at his beloved collection of pornography. He saw me passing by and called me, he asked were I was going.

I told him I was leaving him and the children. He looked at me in disbelief, and then covered his face with one hand while the other curled into a fist. When he looked at me again his eyes were hard as flint, and his face took on a purple tinge as he stood up and flung his chair into the corner.

He called me a whore; obviously he thought that I was leaving him for another man. He accused me of having an affair; he was yelling and screaming horrible insults and shouting so loud that I thought the neighbors would call the police. "Tell me the name of this man, you filthy bitch," he demanded, "or I'll beat you to within an inch of your life."

He got up; put his right hand on his shoulder, his eyes pleading with me, his hand reaching out to grasp my hand as he tried to mouth some words.

He dropped dead on top of a magazine showing a woman wearing only cowboy boots and a hat.

Repulsed, I stared at him as saliva dribbled down his cheek. For the last time I met his eyes, then I turned on my heel and walked out the door.

The Hall on the Green

The local hall on the green in Stradbally catered for almost everybody's needs in the entertainment line. When I was young the words „Community Hall' hadn't entered our vocabulary, as yet, so it was just called 'The Hall'. The Hall catered for everything; Irish dancing lessons, Whist drives, local talent shows, meetings of various committees and of course travelling Drama groups, who tended to put on the same shows every year, Murder in Red Barn, Noreen Bawn, the Croppy Boy and a host of others. We had seen them all so often that we could recite the words with the actors and sometimes we did. Stradbally got so little in the way of strangers or tourists that there was always great excitement and the fact that the players stayed in the town added to it. For us teenagers the biggest excitement of all was the leading man. He played the lead in every production.

When I look back I realise he was a swaggering bottle tanned, bottled blond, bit of a twit who loved himself. Of course we were young and adored him. Who wouldn't with a name like Chick Kaye? We thought he was gorgeous and his name fell off our tongues like honey. Mrs Chick Kaye we would call ourselves with a lot of nudging and laughing. We weren't jealous of each other; we just wanted him to pick one of us. Then the rest of us could bask in reflected glory. It wasn't to be, he always went for the older woman, someone about twenty five.

But for my grandmother, sister and I there was only one night of the week we really looked forward to, the one night that we found ourselves standing outside the hall at seven thirty, filled with expectations of what was to come, and that was Friday night, the night the Man from Enniscorthy delivered the magic of Hollywood to our local hall. It was always an adventure. We never knew what film we were going to see until it started. There was always great speculation as to what the film might be. The boys looking for cowboys and Indians and the girls hoping it would be a love story.

Another part of the adventure was you never knew what time you would be going home. It could be ten thirty or it could be twelve thirty. For instance, his car often broke down on the way from Enniscorthy and we would wait, hail rain or snow, ducking into shops and doorways. He would eventually ring one of the nearby shops asking them to tell us he was on his way.

When he did arrive the screen had to be put up and the projector put in place. It didn't all end there; the film itself could break down. Now, it didn't matter to us if it was Pathe News, we thought that could be scrapped altogether and something else shown in its place.

However he sometimes took advantage of the breakdown, he would have a draw for twenty Sweet Afton cigarettes. There were always a couple of boys from the audience willing to sell the tickets. It you won, and you were lucky enough to have someone with you, you were alright. If not, some adult took them from you telling you that you were too young to smoke.

My grandmother loved the cinema and her favourite film stars were Ronald Coleman and Greer Garson. The film she loved was Random Harvest. I must have seen it about six times with her. Our Man from Enniscorthy wasn't bothered how often he showed a film and we didn't mind either. A very young girl called Margaret O'Brien became famous overnight. She always played sad, tragic roles, being a little waif of a thing anyway, so the whole image suited her. My friend Hazel thought she was the image of her. We teased her about this all the time and she loved it.

As for the night itself, because of the occasional late start and maybe a couple of breakdowns, it was often twelve thirty before we left the hall. Walking home we would meet Sergeant O'Connell stopping cyclists who had no light on their bikes. There would be a hefty fine of a couple of shillings in the Court on the following Tuesday.

The cinema was a huge part of our lives then. Where our heroes and heroines loved, danced, fought, died and saved the Wild West. What young girl wouldn't want to be a ballerina and all the boys wanted to be gunslingers. Our Man from Enniscorthy helped us dream our dreams even if it was only every Friday night.

Times have changed but like everyone else, we thought our times were the best. The admission charge was one shilling and six pence. After two lots of currency change in my lifetime I'm lost. I just haven't a clue how much it would be now.

Tents of Sand

Wailing wind on the horn of Africa
Turning mill grinds a quenchless hope
Judas tree am I, of fruitless care
I roll through a village, tread inner air.

Across the gloom under the plough
Harrow bleeds with rusting stars
Walking with babes, bundles in flight
Beauty lost in solitary place.

Stick insects burrow in the sand
Lips filled with pale clay
Protruding bones, huge eyes, know me
We shall meet no more.

Last winter blackbirds fell from trees
Bare, black babes fall, under summer heat
Eagles circle in my wake
Welcome, heaven meets hell.

Water carriers fear my blade
More than bullets or bombs
Under flags, trumpets, Calvary's relief
No rain yesterday, today, tomorrow's parched

Fog's affliction of Aga,
 Reaper takes no golden corn
I am at each man's table,
Invisible to all.

No laments bring down the rain
No descent on sandy wastes
Mill goes round by radiant moon
Drink the wine, be nourished.

Bless yourself, I have arrived
In the rustling harvest
Of cracked earths dust covering
My steps are soundless on the sand.

Existing where nothing exists
In castle's sand of moon
Arid wind sighs my name
Hunger

Aga; means land of muslins
The radiant moon; is Mohammed
Wine; is the love of God

The Corrib

When May is on the bush
The Corrib beckons pilgrims,
Days are warming in the west,
Anglers check their boxes.

Lines are cleaned, flies tied,
A fever's on my spirit
Another week to go, a hundred miles,
So many patterns still to tie.

The art of fur and feather
Handed down to me, years at the vice,
Stations I must visit, a ritual love,
Split canes put together sing.

I cast myself upon your placid water,
Amidst silver trout a leaping,
In a tranquil place I hear your sounds
With haul of oars at a gentle pace.

Your beauty steals my heart,
When the water boils
I cast, wait for the take,
A great fish to dive
With my heart of dreams.

Wasted

No memoirs wake
Unseal the lid of days.
A life deeds shelved in silent dust,
No photos shrivelling.

Was he fair among sons of earth?
On James Street, gate of ages
Steal on,
Cobbles to commune departed years.

I smell hops, studded boot on stone,
Souls deep voice pours, portrays,
Pale clay of sleepers, French cobbles
In a voyage of absence.

Enrol the dreams on corduroy roads,
Feast of victories' footsteps,
A bloom echoes,
His of Maxim, Vickers spitting lead.

Acoustic shadows torment sleep,
Labyrinth of bell tents,
Thousands of voices ponder
While sweetly tell of life.

Above bivouacs the Somme trench,
Star shells slowly reveal
Impartial rats eating brown or grey
Among stump figures of snags.

Night crews crawl in blackened holes
Sunshine or shadow, in harm's way
Creatures with tin hats exposed,
Shells bursting, slowly stiffening.

Rags of unburied dead, without shroud
Wither on snagged wire, man traps,
Like trawl nets, harvest waves
In all tangled storm, raining shells.

When a whistle blows along the cut
Boiling over the rim, into the heat,
Runaways entranced in craters, lip to lip,
Minds shake in boots, all afraid.

Wearing too much beauty for the grave
Entombed, blowing candles in the shrill blast.
Deaths' duel to win, duty bound,
Youth out of season, drop like ripe fruit.

Without rites, in chalk mud they disappear
No bloom fades your veil of sleep
Sorrow and death cannot enter,
Forget-me-not covered with breath of moss.

Wild array of poppies, nodding,
In the kingdom of the tomb.
My eye has not seen a chalk face,
My ear knows not a distant gun.

I bend my knee to dig
Begetter of our heritage,
Minstrel, born to roam,
In long lost shade.

Wheel crushed hearts, sanctified,
Death's victory, a slitted grin.
You looked at bubble-frothed mouths,
Heard plop-plop, verminous breath.

Smelt flush of un-genial air,
All buried long ago, though buried.
Mind treasures silently unfold.
Thought draws my fond affection.

Moseying in their victory, frozen dance,
Summoned on cobbles gone soft.
Mankind grew wicked,
Wine bubbles on my tongue.

Anthony

It was a bright day in late November 1965 and the view across Kenmare Bay truly magnificent, when my brother, Anthony was born in the District Hospital, in Kenmare. The local hospital looked out on a panoramic view of patchwork fields, Kenmare bay and the majestic mountains of Kerry.

Earlier that day mammy had asked my sister, Kitty, who had just turned fourteen to go across the street to the neighbours, and ask could one of them drive her to the hospital.

"Are you sick, mammy?" kitty had anxiously enquired. She could see that our mother, Joan, was in pain.

"I will be alright, Kitty," mammy reassured her, "I just need to go to the hospital for a while. Go on now, like a good girl," she encouraged.

Kitty obediently hastened across the street as requested. She was concerned for her mother. She had never seen her like this. A request like this was alien to her young mind.

When Kitty left the house, mammy turned to my eldest sister, "Jenny, go to the District Nurse's house and tell her I have to go to the hospital,"

Jenny did as she was bidden, though worried about leaving her mother who was obviously in a lot of pain; she got on her bike and cycled as fast as her legs could go, mindful to be careful as her mother instructed.

As she cycled she wondered how they would get word to our father, who because of trouble with his hips, was in the orthopaedic hospital in Cork.

As my mother, Joan, entered the front door of the hospital she said a silent prayer to Our Lady to give her strength, and asked for the safe delivery of her child. She was worried about the baby's birth. This was her ninth child and she was forty six years of age.

She reached the waiting area, where the midwife welcomed her kindly.

The labour was short and mammy was grateful for that.

"You have a lovely, baby boy," the midwife informed her, "with a good strong cry and a healthy colour. This is excellent news," she said as she placed the newborn baby into my mother's arms.

Mammy was relieved and filled with great joy, to have her beautiful baby boy, with golden hair and blue eyes placed in her arms. She thanked the midwife for her kindness to her, and then quietly said a prayer of thanks to the Sacred Heart, and Our Lady, for their help.

"Have you decided on a name for him, Mrs O'Sullivan?" The midwife inquisitively enquired.

"We like the name Anthony," mammy replied, as Saint Anthony was one of her favourite saints. He would help protect her little son and keep him safe, and as she gazed down at his downy head, she determined that she would never allow anyone to shorten his name to Tony or Ant.

The midwife phoned the orthopaedic hospital in Cork and spoke to our father. The news of another boy thrilled him to the core. The O'Sullivan name will live on, he thought delightedly. O'Sullivan and Sons sounded really good to him. Boys could take over the business in the town, the farm, and the harness making skills he inherited from his father, Eugene, who was known throughout the county for his expertise in making harnesses.

The whole ward congratulated him on the safe arrival of his baby boy. Every time he thought of his new son that day he smiled. He was really looking forward to meeting him.

The nurses had great difficulty feeding Anthony. He had a poor suck. They tried various methods. Finally, they came up with a solution for him. With great patience and skill, milk was gently and carefully spooned into his mouth, little and often, until he got stronger and was able to suck by himself.

There was a great welcome for Anthony from all his brothers and sisters. We couldn't contain our excitement, imagine, a new baby brother! We went to the hospital at visiting time.

"Oh, mammy, he is so tiny." Margaret said.

"Can I hold him?" Theresa asked.

"Best let him rest, love, he is tired," our mother lovingly said.

Jenny could see how pale and tired our kind mother looked. So she firmly ushered us out of the room with a promise that we could visit mammy again tomorrow.

We pleaded to stay a little longer, but Jenny wouldn't hear of it.

"Mammy is tired now and needs to sleep, but I promise I will bring you all here again after school tomorrow," she stated.

We reluctantly left the ward with sad faces and tears in our eyes. Home was not the same without our mother and father.

After we left, mammy found herself growing progressively weaker. Her blood loss seemed to be very heavy, but she thought it was because of her age. She reckoned it would settle down. She didn't want to trouble the nurses, they were very busy. She could hear lots of activity out in the corridor and wished she could rouse herself to go and tell them how she felt. At this stage she had a ringing in her ears, her vision was blurred and she found it hard to focus.

Luckily, at that moment, a nurse came into her room to check on her, saw the situation and called for help. Mammy was haemorrhaging; she passed out as the doctor was called. Thankfully, they had got her in time, her recovery was very slow and she didn't make it home for Christmas that year.

I will never forget the day she found out that Anthony had Down syndrome. He was two years of age and looked to be the same as any other little boy his age. She had arrived home from the Doctor in Kenmare.

Myself, and the majority of my other siblings were present. My brother, Gene, was doing his geography homework on the kitchen table. Jenny was also doing her homework beside Gene. The young twins, Edward and Timothy, were happily playing with building blocks along with Anthony. It was my turn to do the wash up that day, I was washing the dishes. Margaret and Christine were looking after the shop my parents ran, and my father was sitting by the fire, reading the paper. It was a typical day in the O'Sullivan household.

Mammy arrived home with a strange look on her face that I could not comprehend. Her gaze was transfixed on Anthony. A tear trickled down her right cheek. My mother was a strong, capable woman, whom I'd never seen cry. This was an unusual sight for me and the family.

"Are you alright, mammy?" I asked. No answer came, just more tears. The rest of us shared an uneasy and confused looks at each other. Then the words came out, slowly and quietly.

"The Doctor said Anthony is a Mongol."

Back in the 1960s a Mongol was the term we now refer to as Down syndrome. At this period in time, Down syndrome was not as fully understood, as it is today. The facilities and care we have now were not available then.

Confusion spread across the room. Gene was looking at his geography map and he asked inquisitively, "how could Anthony be a Mongol? He was born in Kenmare, not Mongolia. He's Irish, surely ... He's Irish," Gene kept repeating.

"He'll have to go in to institutional care," mammy said, her voice barely a whisper.

"No mammy," I blurted out, "I'll become a nurse and *I'll* mind him."

As the days went by, good hearted people advised my mother to put Anthony into care, to protect the marriage prospects of the rest of her children. At the time having a Mongol in the family would deem the family as inferior.

Thank God she didn't yield to such pressure; she was a strong, resilient woman, who had gone through a lot in her life. She had given birth to nine children, and lost one, Danny, from a cot death at two years of age. As well as rearing us she took in two of our cousins, both girls, who had lost their mother.

As Anthony grew older he was enrolled in the local primary school, to attempt life as a normal child. Anthony was on constant surveillance by the headmaster, he was concerned that Anthony would be disruptive, and wouldn't be able to keep up with the children. Fortunately the headmaster found Anthony to be placid, gentle, caring and loving, and he grew very fond of him.

My mother and the headmaster were ahead of their time, they fought for Anthony to have the life he deserved, instead of being sent off to an institute, and never seen again by his loved ones.

He enjoyed many happy, fulfilled years in Kenmare. He got his first job there in the Butcher's shop, down the street where we loved. He made great friends in Kenmare; everyone was very fond of him.

Mammy and Anthony had a great social life together; they went away on weekends with the Kerry Down Syndrome Society. They took trips to Knock, in County Mayo, and trips to Medjugorje, and Bosnia-Herzegovina. Anthony also enjoyed trips with his parents, to the various households of his married siblings. He was never seen as a burden to the family, only a great joy.

I write this account as a tribute to our Mother who died 12th March 2011. She had the vision to see what society didn't. She saw Anthony to be just as capable as the next child. She knew it was in Anthony's best interest, and in the family's, to be raised in a loving, caring home, in his community where he received much love and kindness.

Biographies

Rosemary Finnegan

Rosemary, originally from Portarlington, has been living in Portlaoise with her husband, Liam, since 1972. Rosemary has always had an interest in the Arts and has been painting for many years. She is one of the founder members of the Laois Writer's Group, which was formed in 1994. Rosemary's short stories have been published in two of the Laois Anthologies, and her work has appeared in "Road to Mountmellick".

Frank Parker

Frank is a retired Engineer. He spent most of his working life in England where he was employed by UK based multi-national companies. He always wanted to write but has only found the freedom to do so since retiring to Ireland in October 2006. Formerly resident in Portlaoise, he now lives with Freda, his wife of 48 years, in Stradbally.

A member of Laois Writer's Group since 2010 he says the support and encouragement he has received from other group members has been invaluable. "I could never have completed a whole novel without the confidence that group membership has given me. Even if it never gets published the experience has been extremely satisfying." Opening passages from his novel are included in this anthology under the title "Leave Taking".

Myra O'Brien

Myra was born in Waterford, but when she was very young her family moved to Portlaoise, where she has lived since then. Myra is married to Stephen, with a grown up family, she is a member of the Literature Studies Group in Portlaoise, and recently joined the Laois Writer's Group to pursue her interest in writing. Myra is delighted to contribute to this anthology.

Maeve Heneghan

Maeve is a native of County Dublin. After living and working in China for two years, she moved back to Ireland and County Laois. She has been living in Portlaoise with her husband and daughter for the past eight years. An avid reader, Maeve has been writing poetry and short stories for several years, and has had work published online and in print. Maeve is a member of the Laois Writer's Group.

Margaret Cotter

Margaret, a native of Portlaoise, is married with one son who resides in Dublin. She is chairperson, and also a founder member, of the Laois Writer's Group. Margaret, who writes short stories and poetry, has been published in the Laois Anthologies, Waterford Review, Force Ten Journal Mayo. Roscommon Writer's Anthology, the National Library of Poetry and recently in Writing 4 All anthology 2011.

Her work has been broadcast on Dublin Community Radio, Gay Byrne Radio Show, Midland Radio Three and Live at Three, RTE. Her first collection of poetry "Lines of our Lives" was published in 2003. She won the Molly Keane Memorial Creative Writing Award in 2006. Margaret now lives outside Cullohill, in County Laois.

Mary Carmody

Mary is a native of Portlaoise, and resides at Rossleighan with her husband, Dan. Mary has two grown up children living away. She has had a lifelong interest in art and the written word. When she retired, Mary decided to pursue her interests. To that effect she has joined the Literature Studies Group, and become a member of the Laois Writer's Group. These stories are her first published work.

Graciela Ryan

Graciela was born in Mexico City, where she studied Law. She moved to Ireland to learn English. To pursue her love of English, Graciela joined the Literature Studies Group in Portlaoise. She enjoys writing, her short stories and poems give an insight from the point of view of a Mexican living in Europe. She resides in Portlaoise with her husband and children, where she attends the Laois Writer's Group.

Lal Curtin

Lal is originally from Athy but is very happy to be living in Portlaoise. A member of the Laois Writer's Group since 1995, she enjoys the support, encouragement and company of the other members. Lal's poetry and short stories have been published in the Laois Anthologies and she had a story published in an Anthology called, "Road to Mountmellick". Lal's writing draws on her vast experience of life.

Tom Moore

Tom was born and grew up in Dublin. He moved to Rathdowney, County Laois in 1973. He is married with five children. A plumber by trade Tom has been a member of the Laois Writer's Group for the last ten years.

Tom is a poet, and his work has been published in the Laois anthologies. His poetry has been broadcast on local radio, and he has read for Amnesty International in Portlaoise. Tom spends a lot of his time raising money for charities, like the Children's Hospital, Crumlin, Irish Kidney Association and the Cuisle Centre, Portlaoise. His hobbies include fishing, motor cycling and playing the guitar, he also carves in bog oak.

Mary Conway

Mary, originally from Kenmare, County Kerry, went to London in 1975 to train as a nurse. After graduating, she worked for several years in England, before returning to Ireland and Portlaoise, where she works as a midwife.

Married to Michael with three children, Mary enjoys walking, swimming, cycling, art and Parish activities. Mary is a member of the Ten AM Choir and a member of the Baptism Team. She has recently joined the Laois Writers Group to pursue her interest in writing. This is her first published work.

List of Sponsors

Laois Co Council, Portlaoise

Anthony O'Sullivan's Siblings, Portlaoise/Kenmare

VHI Staff Charities Committee, Dublin

Francesca Restaurant, Portlaoise

Egans Restaurant, Portlaoise

Frank Parker, Stradbally

Gerry Brown Jewellers, Portlaoise

Parkside Chemist, Portlaoise

Miriam Finnegan, Portlaoise

Adam's Chemist, Portlaoise

Fairgreen Chemist, Portlaoise

Mr Hosam El-Kininy Consultant Obstetrician, Gynaecologist, FRcos, Frcsed, MRCPI, Dip. Ultrasound, RCR/RCOG General Hospital, Portlaoise

Miriam Doyle, General Hospital Portlaoise

Doctors, Midwives, Nurses, Care Assistants, Multi Skilled Attendants, Ward Clerk, Porters, General Hospital Portlaoise

Parentcraft, General Hospital Portlaoise

Lal Curtin, Portlaoise

GW Reid Associates Chartered Accountants, Prestwick, Scotland

Ciarain ORourke, Portlaoise

Tom Moore, Rathdowney

TT Ramrods MCC, Templetoughy

Angelo Marsella Smart Energy Installations, Dublin

Moore Family, Rathdowney

Collins Removal, Portlaoise

continued overleaf >

Sponsors cointunued . . .

Midland Hardware, Rathdowney

Egans Off License, Portlaoise

Catherine and John Fitzpatrick , Rathdowney

David and Jean Moore, Rathdowney

John OMalley's Publican, Rathdowney

Paddy Fitzpatrick, Rathdowney

John Moore, Portlaoise

Flynn's Medical Hall, Rathdowney

Greg Fennell, Portlaoise

Sean Maher, Rathdowney

PJ O'Brien, Portlaoise

Signatures

Signatures